don't cramp my style

don't cramp my style

stories about that
time of the month

EDITED BY LISA ROWE FRAUSTINO

simon & schuster books for young readers
New York London Toronto Sydney

BS

SIMON & SCHUSTER BOOKS FOR YOUNG READERS
An imprint of Simon & Schuster Children's Publishing Division
1230 Avenue of the Americas, New York, New York 10020

Book design by O'Lanso Gabbidon

The text for this book is set in Filosofia.
Manufactured in the United States of America
10 9 8 7 6 5 4 3 2 1

CIP data for this book is available from the Library of Congress.
ISBN 0-689-85882-5

contents

don't cramp my style

snapshots in blood

by Michelle H. Martin

five

my mother led a Girl Scout troop for most of my childhood. One year, one of the girls in her troop got pregnant. Since that was rare in the 1970s, and since my mother didn't want this one scout to have a bad influence on the others, she put her out of the troop. Devastated, the girl sat on the front porch of our house every day the Girl Scout troop met, hoping Mom would let her back in. But my mother was adamant.

Eventually the other girls in the troop started to beg Mom on the girl's behalf. She relented, but only on one condition: that the whole troop and the pregnant scout watch a film together about the birthing experience. They all agreed, and all of them got their parents' permission to watch it.

I don't remember the name of the film, but as I sat in the living room on the lap of one of the scouts, peeking out from behind my hands, I do remember the woman's screaming when the baby came out . . . the gush of blood . . . the afterbirth flooding out of her . . . the bloody, screaming baby . . . feeling grateful that the film didn't come with smells.

The rest of the girls graduated from high school without getting pregnant.

So did I.

seven

Connie, a fifteen-year-old friend of my brother, grabbed me by the hand, pulled me into our tiny bathroom, sat me in the corner behind the door on the blue-and-white tiles, pulled down her jeans and underwear, and sat on the toilet. Immediately the bathroom filled with a smell that I had never encountered before and hoped never to again. She pulled her bloody sanitary napkin from her underwear, swung it around to face me, and said, "Your turn is coming. You're going to do this too." As I sat there, wondering how to hold my breath without her knowing, I sincerely hoped she was wrong. *But if she's right and I am going to bleed,* I thought, *I can't possibly let myself smell like this.*

eleven

I had my first period in Kentucky in early summer. The next month, when I packed to go to Girl Scout camp, my mother gave me minipads to take. I didn't know what a problem that would be until it was too late.

The second week of a two-week session, my unit packed up to go primitive camping on the outskirts of camp property. I loved primitive camping, even though we had to dig our own latrines, got sand in everything, and fought bugs the whole time. But this time, I felt uneasy about being so far from a flushing toilet because my second period had started full blast a day or two into the camp session, and it hadn't stopped yet. The minipads were getting dangerously low and doing little to soak up the river between my legs.

A week into my period, we hiked out to the primitive site. For some reason, I hadn't been able to fix my mouth to ask any of my counselors for more or bigger pads. And the second night out, a bout of cramps doubled me over. I lay moaning on my sleeping bag until one of the counselors got me up to hike me back to camp and to the infirmary. The nurse figured out what was wrong with me, although I didn't tell her, and after giving me a heating pad, something for the pain, and time to sleep it off, she loaded me up with a box of pads to get me through this period, which ended up lasting eleven days.

When I got home, my mom dumped my footlocker in front of the washing machine as she always did, with the intention of washing everything in it, since she never knew what things might crawl out of it after two weeks of camp. When she pulled out the favorite plaid pants I had been wearing on the trek from primitive camping to the infirmary and saw my bloody explosion, she gasped in surprise and said, "Michelle, what *happened*?"

"You gave me *minipads*, Mom!"

That was the last time she ever bought minipads.

thirteen

The next summer at Girl Scout camp, my best friend, Robin, and I made a new friend. We were no urbanites ourselves, but Tee, our new friend, was from the "serious country!" She kept amazing us with things she hadn't done and things she hadn't seen. One day during rest hour, the three of us traipsed out of our canvas platform tent, and Tee prepared to learn from us something her mother had refused to teach her: how to use tampons.

Armed with a fresh tampon, Tee shuffled into the bathroom, slammed the creaky wooden door to the stall, and awaited our directions. Already collapsing into giggles over the whole situation, Robin and I blared step-by-step instructions to Tee. Once we figured she had to have it in, we asked her how it felt. A distressed-sounding Tee responded: **"It's in the wrong hole!"** After Robin and I recovered from another fit of laughter, we told her that unless she stuck it up her butt, there's no way to put it in the wrong hole. "There's only one place for it to go." And whether she was just enjoying making us laugh, or whether the effect of the tampon on her was real, Tee came waddling out of the toilet stall walking as if three quarters of the tampon were still hanging out. I think that was the last time either of us tried to teach someone else how to use a tampon.

fourteen

I got on the bus one cold morning during my freshman year of high school. I hated riding the bus, and this particular morning reminded me why. Halfway to school, two boys started loud-talking each other, and soon enough, it turned into a fistfight. Not wanting to get hit, I moved out of my seat and sat farther back. The fight got so bad that the bus driver stopped the bus and put one of the boys off.

When I got to school, I walked into my favorite class, Honors English, took my jacket off, and got ready to sit down. Mrs. Pressley, my English teacher whom I adored, walked over to me as if she had something urgent to say, got right up in my face, and asked me quietly, "Michelle, are you having your period today?" I wouldn't have been more surprised if she had slapped me.

"Yes."

"Well, I think you'd better go to the restroom and check your skirt."

She picked up my jacket, helped me wrap it around my waist, and I walked out of the classroom and down the hall to the nearest bathroom. I could feel my classmates staring at me, and all I could think of was how many of them had seen blood on my skirt when I walked from the bus and probably laughed at me rather than told me.

Once I got to the bathroom, I was both relieved and

baffled to realize that I hadn't bled through my clothes even though the spot was undeniably there. I then remembered the fight on the bus and decided that one of the boys on the bus must have bled on my seat, and when I sat back down, I sat right in the bloody puddle.

I cleaned up the mess, went back to class, and after class went up to Mrs. Pressley to thank her for telling me about my skirt and to explain what I figured had happened. Still mortified about the blood but eternally grateful that Mrs. Pressley had told me instead of letting me walk around school all day like that, I left English class.

twenty-nine

Finishing my Ph.D. in English, I decided to write my dissertation on novels that girls read that talk about menstruation, and those goofy films that girls watch in fifth grade that supposedly teach them about puberty.

There's really no way to describe the expressions I see and the responses I get when middle-aged men ask me over dinner, "So what's your dissertation topic?"

Of course, I tell them.

thirty

Nina, the daughter of Connie who dragged me into the bathroom at the age of seven, gets her first period. I take her and Domonique, my niece, who is also Nina's good friend, out for ice cream to celebrate.

thirty-three

At the end of the summer, thirteen-year-old Domonique tells me that she has taught herself to use tampons at my house. I am spared.

thirty-four

One night, in the middle of teaching Adolescent Literature, I realized with dismay that, if I kept bleeding at the rate I was bleeding at that moment, I would be sitting in a pool of my own blood long before class was over.

And I was.

Somehow I finished teaching class without getting up out of my seat, waited until all of my students had gone, and then sat there until the halls cleared. Fortunately, it was a night class, and few students were around. I got myself across the hall to the bathroom just to confirm that I was indeed soaked, then made it back to my office, into my truck (sitting on a towel), and back home.

Until six months later when I had surgery to have the uterine fibroids removed that were making me bleed so much, I wore black pants every day of my period . . . just in case. In the meantime, I figured that this must be the male gods' way of getting back at me for my dissertation.

thirty-six

I am lying on my bed, wearing a set of earphones and looking intently to see if my husband, Glenn, who is also wearing a set of earphones, is hearing what I'm hearing. A fast, pulsating wave. I see an inkling of recognition on his face, then a big grin: "That's her heartbeat, isn't it?"

"Yeah." And we listen until the baby turns and we can't hear it anymore.

This new toy, this fetal monitor, is giving us an audible window into Amelia's world: her kicks, her hiccups, the sloshing sounds of my amniotic fluid moving around her. Her heartbeat.

The stains on my favorite plaid pants at eleven, the humiliation of having my favorite teacher tell me about my bloody skirt at fourteen, sitting in my own puddle of blood in class at thirty-four all amount to nothing when I lie in bed with these earphones. Inside this basketball-sized lump that is part of me is a little person with a heart and lungs who stretches and yawns, and who will come into the world in less than ten weeks with ovaries that contain all the eggs she'll ever have. And one day, she and I and all of her closest friends will have an ice cream party to celebrate her first bleeding. Then I will know that *my* snapshots in blood will have come full circle, and hers will have just begun.

In Joan Elizabeth Goodman's story, "The Czarevna of Muscovy," the wise old Baba Irina tells young Katya: "You must learn how to set your spirit free even as you remain in the Kremlin. For you have no choice but to live the life you are given." In a sense, this same theme runs throughout the stories in *Don't Cramp My Style*. Whether the young menstruous woman is destined to become the ruler of Russia, as is Katya, or whether she will become a breeder for a young man on a nearby plantation to produce more human chattel for a slave master, as is Salome in Alice McGill's "Moon Time Child," all women must live the lives they are given and learn to be at home in their menstruating bodies. This process of learning to live with bodies that participate in cycles beyond our control sometimes gives us cause to celebrate, sometimes to laugh, sometimes to mourn, and sometimes to wonder.

In Pat Brisson's "Taking Care of Things," she tells a humorous tale of Carly Pender's negotiating having her period one day in high school when circumstances conspire against her making it to a restroom in a timely manner. Wanting to impress the boy of her dreams as well as the editor-in-chief of the school newspaper who keeps giving her crappy writing assignments, Carly has an encounter in the hallway that solves more than just the problem of what to do about her period. David Lubar's protagonist in "The Heroic Quest of Douglas MacGawain" offers a male conundrum concerning menstruation: What's a guy to do when his girlfriend sends him to the store to get soda and a box of tampons? Evade the request? Or become the feminist hero she expects him to be and bring home what she wants?

Alice McGill's "Moon Time Child" and Dianne Ochiltree's "The Women's House" shift the mood of the volume. These contemplative pieces depict diverse cultural contexts for menstruation in which menarche serves an important social function—for better or worse. The poignant journal entries of young slave Salome reveal how a girl's first bleeding signaled to the slave owner that she was ready to mate, even if the girl felt unready and unwilling to serve her master in this capacity. Sparrow-Song, on the other hand, learns about menstruation and birth at the same time and comes to realize that both of these female events keep relationships between women strong and give them a time away from men to nurture one another. Goodman's "The Czarevna of Muscovy" highlights the opposite end of the social and economic spectrum, as we discover what menarche means for Katya, the future ruler of Russia, who longs to dance in the streets as the common people do but who must keep herself apart in order to take her proper place in society.

With Lisa Rowe Fraustino's story, the volume turns its attention to the dark side of menstruating—the stories of lives touched and altered irreversibly by menstrual blood. The unnamed protagonist of Lisa Rowe Fraustino's "Sleeping Beauty," seems to make monumental efforts to detach herself from her body—until her body refuses to allow her to ignore it any longer. Joyce McDonald's "Transfusion" gives us a glimpse into what menstruation means for one mentally ill character, Evie, as she helps protagonist Mona realize that she still has options in her primary relationship that she might not have if she were not sane herself. This connection between menstruation and mental illness continues in Han Nolan's "Maroon," in which the early connection that the main character's promiscuous cousin has given her between death and menstrual bleeding eventually compromises this young girl's sanity.

The volume's three final stories tell of important events that variously signal what it means to enter womanhood. Deborah Heiligman's "Ritual Purity" tells a contemporary Jewish coming-of-age story of transformation that also relates a teen's initiation into a positive female community. Miriam must help to save the life of her aunt, who has miscarried, before she realizes the value of her own life. Only then do her family and her religion begin to mean anything to her. Julie Stockler's "Losing It" tells a hippie story of Jessie's first sexual experience—which happens while she is menstruating. Teasing from her friends about her sexual encounter on the beach is the least of her worries when it's over. Linda Oatman High's "The Uterus Fairy" conveys a story that most women will recognize: Chelsea must live through several agonizing days, wondering whether or not she is pregnant as she promises God and all of the celestial powers she can recall that if she gets her period only this once, she will never complain about it ever again and will make wiser choices hereafter.

Taken as a whole, these stories of young womanhood illustrate that while menstruation can mean vastly different things to women at various times in our lives, this physiological commonality gives us a lived experience worth sharing.

taking care of things
by Pat Brisson

"**melanie**?" I called to my editor-in-chief before she could slip away to first period. I was standing outside Ms. Turner's class in front of the bulletin board with our next assignments on it. Or at least with *everyone else's* next assignment on it, since my name wasn't on the list.

Melanie turned toward me, swinging her shiny black hair over her shoulder as though auditioning for a shampoo commercial. She had a smile that didn't reach her eyes—all teeth and no heart. "Yes?" she asked with a look that seemed surprised that I had been bold enough to call her by name. She'd have been even more surprised if I called her the rhyming variation of her last name—Fritchie—that I use in my imagined conversations with her.

"The assignment list," I told her. "I'm not up there."

"Ohhhh . . ." She drew the word out, stalling for time,

so I realized she had no idea who I was, which she finally admitted. "And you are . . . ?"

"Carly Pender," I told her. Ace investigative reporter, I thought to myself but didn't say out loud. Ever since that report I did back in fourth grade on Nellie Bly, a famous female investigative reporter of the late nineteenth century, I'd known that was my destiny. I was forever making up lists of story ideas—not the obvious ones about winning teams and honor students, but the less-obvious ones about the challenges faced by Rose Brownmiller, a blind student who maneuvers around school with her guide dog; or the silent hopes of the group that hangs out on the footbridge before first bell, smoking their last cigarettes of the morning; or the dirty little secret I keep hearing about how wrestlers and football players don't get suspended in season no matter what rule they break.

"Oh, right! Carly!" she said, although I could tell she had no recollection of me.

Now, it's true this is only November of my freshman year, but still, I've attended every editorial meeting that's been called. I've dutifully handed in the less-than-stellar assignments I've been given: What percentage of the student body prefers fruit juices to bottled water, and how the turf management team feels the football field is holding up this season. It's not as though she has a staff of hundreds. You'd think she'd at least remember who I was.

Melanie checked the assignment sheet. Big surprise—my name still wasn't there. "This is the list of assigned articles for the newspaper," she told me in a voice someone might use with a Russian immigrant who'd mistaken the sheet for a list of subway stops. "Only people on the newspaper staff are listed here."

I pressed my lips together to prevent the wrong words from slipping out and inhaled slowly. "I know what it is," I told her. "I'm on the newspaper staff. I was wondering why I wasn't given an assignment."

"Oh, you're *on* the newspaper staff! Well then, Okay. No problem. I'll get an assignment to you before the end of the day." She smiled again—that glistening, heartless smile—and sauntered off before I thought to ask where we'd meet. I rushed to Earth Science class, muttering satisfying comebacks under my breath.

I pretended to pay attention and take notes, but I was only vaguely aware of Mr. Bledsoe going on about red tides, describing how bodies of water can turn red because of microscopic plants mysteriously increasing by the millions. What I was really doing was trying to calm down. Melanie had totally shaken my confidence. If my own *editor* couldn't remember me and my work, how was I ever going to make it as a journalist?

Ulcers run in my family. So ever since third grade, when my mother had taught me relaxation exercises, I'd trained myself to escape that churned-up, ready-to-boil-over sensation with a pleasant visualization. My pleasant visualization of choice these days was Doug Fulmer.

Doug is a dark-haired, hard-bodied soccer player who also plays saxophone in the jazz band. When my oboe-playing friend, Jessica, told me this, I seriously considered taking up the clarinet in spite of the fact that I am genetically unmusical. Then I came to my senses.

Since I'll never be in the band, I have to make do with attending all the soccer games where the sight of him on the field—all hot and sweaty and breathing hard—kicks my thermostat up another notch. He's not like the football jocks who think they're God's gifts to females. Doug Fulmer doesn't seem to realize he's hot, which makes him all the more attractive to me. Unfortunately he's a senior and doesn't even know I exist.

So there I was in Earth Science, Mr. Bledsoe droning on in the background, enjoying my recurring daydream in which Doug and I are on a field trip to the Statue of Liberty when a sudden hurricane forces an immediate evacuation. Doug and I are in the museum, enjoying a thousand and one variations of Liberty Enlightening the World rendered in plastic banks, postcards, telephones, and beach towels, and miss the announcement that everyone has left the island. We are accidentally left behind, where we soon discover an intense attraction to one another that cannot be denied. (I got that line off the back of a romance novel at Redson's Pharmacy and love all the passion it so subtly suggests.)

I'm very good at visualization. I spent the majority of that period imagining Doug and me doing pleasant things to each other on Liberty Island, with an occasional tune-in to Mr. Bledsoe and the mysteries of the red tide. By the end of class I was feeling very wet. I was pretty sure it had nothing to do with phytoplankton.

In English, Mrs. Harding told us we could use the time in class to work on our poem analyses. We have to do one every month. I was doing two pages on Alfred Noyes's use of color in "The Highwayman." I got down to work right away, imagining myself as the red-lipped daughter plaiting a dark red love knot into my long black hair and seeing my lover, who looked amazingly like Doug Fulmer in my imagination, wearing those breeches of brown doeskin that "fitted with never a wrinkle." I believe a student should enjoy her schoolwork, and I was thinking, *Ooooh, baby, you can clash in my dark inn yard anytime you please*, and trying to suppress a moan, when it occurred to me that maybe I was a little *too* wet. *Is this more than just me responding to my imaginings*, I wondered. *Is this the middle of my cycle maybe, or worse, the start of my period?* My periods are so wildly unpredictable, it could have been either.

I doodled a calendar in my notebook, trying to pinpoint how long it had been since the last time. The best I could figure, it had been either three or four weeks, since I knew I got it on a Friday and here it was Friday again. Then I sneezed—three times in a row—and I felt that warm gush that could only mean one thing. I had played my Female Dire Emergency Card in this class last week when what I'd really wanted was a break from being bored to death by Mrs. Harding's monthly grammar lesson—this one on identifying subordinate clauses—so since class was almost over, I decided to wait it out. I crossed my legs, tightened the appropriate muscles as hard as I could, and thanked myself for having had enough luck to wear black pants this morning.

Ten minutes later I was out of my seat and heading toward the second-floor west girls' room. I had a test in algebra next class and couldn't be late. Ordinarily getting a pass from Mr. Kosun wouldn't be a problem, but at the start of the year, he'd made it very clear that no one left class during a test unless they were carried out feet first. I had three minutes—well, less than that now—but thought I'd be okay if there wasn't a line for the four available stalls.

Just my luck, the CAREFUL! WET FLOOR! sign was propped in the open doorway. I could see Mr. Selagio, one of the maintenance men, cleaning up what, from my spot in the hallway, smelled like vomit. If it had been one of the maintenance *women*, I would have gone in anyway. But the idea of me standing there sticking money in the feminine care items vending machine and then slipping into a stall with Mr. Selagio working a few feet away was more than I cared to deal with. The hall was crowded. No way could I make it to the other girls' room and still be on time for Algebra.

Okay, Carly, I told myself, trying to control the panic I was beginning to feel, you can take care of things after math class. Just keep pulling in those muscles and try not to laugh, cough, or sneeze.

Luckily I'm pretty good at math, so the test wasn't that difficult, but my mind kept drifting back to the problem between my legs and distracted me enough to keep me from working as quickly as I normally would have. To make matters worse, my vivid imagination created ridiculous scenarios: me rushing down the hallway when a sudden gush bursts from me right in the path of Melanie Fritchie, my next assignment in her hand, who slips in it and falls, cracking her head on the floor; or me running into Rose Brownmiller and her Seeing Eye dog, Henry, who follows my trail of blood down the hallway, leaving poor Rose stranded and unable to find her way to Spanish class; or me running into Doug Fulmer and him noticing the trail of blood (and Henry) behind me, asking, "Did you cut your leg or something?" It was enough to make me break out in a cold sweat and have trouble breathing. I dropped my pencil so I'd have an excuse to bend over and check to see if I was bleeding through yet, but so far I was okay. When the bell rang I still had two problems left (plus the one between my legs) and had to hand in the test uncompleted.

I figured Mr. Selagio would be finished in the girls' room by now, but rather than take the chance (what if there was an *epidemic* of vomiting girls on second floor west today?), I decided to hit the girls' room on the other end of the hall. I breathed a sigh of relief when I saw it was open and started fishing in my purse for change for the vending machine. I found a quarter, slid it into the slot and pulled the lever. Nothing happened. I pulled again. Still nothing. I tried another quarter. This time the lever jammed. I banged the machine and swore at it for good measure, tried the lever again and swore one last time. Usually there would have been other girls in there I could have begged from, but today, for some reason, I was alone.

I sighed, went into a stall, folded up a bunch of toilet paper, and took care of things the best I could. I wished I could just throw my bloody underpants away, but I didn't have time to take them off and besides, I needed them to help hold the toilet paper in place. I figured I could get a pass in World Cultures for sure and go to yet another girls' room.

What I hadn't counted on was having a substitute and worse luck, it was Mrs. Woodson, who thought all kids were out to take advantage of her, and who warned us every time she subbed that "I *never* give out bathroom passes, so don't even bother asking." She prodded us through a review of world religions and I silently prayed to God, Allah, Buddha, and Yahweh that I not bleed through and totally embarrass myself.

My aunt Carrie, whom I was named after and who has some pretty crazy ideas sometimes, once said that women wear red when they have their periods as an unconscious announcement to the world that they are fertile and proud of it. I wondered if guys knew this and was so creeped out by the possibility that I didn't wear red for over a year. I told myself I didn't believe her, and the fact that this morning I'd grabbed a red sweater from my bedroom floor was just a coincidence. Just the same I was glad I had worn it so I could take it off now and sit on it.

I managed to get through the next forty-five minutes, but not without the realization that the object of all my prayers was perhaps too male to completely understand my predicament. So I spent about fifteen minutes trying to recall the names of goddesses from Greek mythology—Hera, Athena, and Aphrodite were the ones I came up with—on the off-chance that they were in a position to answer supplications. I shot out of there before the bell had finished ringing, heading toward the stairwell, figuring I'd get to the girls' room on the first floor since my next class was down there anyway.

It has always struck me as entirely reasonable for kids who are on crutches to get out of class a few minutes early in order to get to their next classes without getting run down by the pack. So the last thing I was expecting was to get stuck behind someone on crutches. I mean, there I was, sucking in my breath as if that would somehow reverse the direction of flow, and hurrying along, but with smaller than usual steps, afraid that the critical wad of toilet paper would come unlodged, when suddenly I found myself behind someone on crutches. But not just anyone on crutches. No, as unbelievable as it seemed—and it made me question if there was any justice in the universe at all—I got stuck behind Rose Brownmiller. Rose Brownmiller *on crutches*! I hadn't even known she'd broken her leg, but here she was now in a cast up to her thigh.

She was carrying a backpack with one shoulder strap twisted, so she'd been unable to put it on correctly. This meant she was wearing the pack on only one shoulder. If she'd been wearing it on the shoulder away from Henry, her guide dog, this would have been less of a problem. But she was wearing it on the shoulder near Henry, and because she was a little bent over from using the crutches, it kept sliding down, banging Henry in the head and knocking against the crutch and nearly wiping her out completely. Poor Henry let out a little whimper each time he got conked on the noggin. Then Rose had to stop walking, readjust her crutch, pull her pack up to her shoulder, say a few comforting words to Henry, take another step, and do everything all over again. This was actually painful to watch.

I was getting wetter by the minute and felt like I had completely soaked through the toilet paper already, but Rose was too hard to ignore. I gave up hope of ever getting to the girls' room and decided I'd help Rose instead and just cut the rest of my classes and go home and take care of things in peace.

I tiny-stepped my way up to her, my thighs pressed firmly together. Rose had dropped her backpack in order to comfort Henry, who had just gotten hit in the head again. "Rose?" I said to her. "My name's Carly Pender. I'd be happy to help you carry your backpack, if you'd like some help." Rose and Henry turned in my direction. Rose smiled. Henry sniffed. And before I knew it, his nose was headed straight toward my crotch, drawn by the smell of fresh blood. Holy Aphrodite! Could it possibly get any worse than this? I tried to distract him, stroking his head, murmuring, "You're a good dog, aren't you, Henry?" thinking *Ple-e-e-ase be a good dog and stay out of my crotch!* I bent over to put some space between us, angling my butt as far away from him as possible while I reached for the backpack.

But as I leaned down, my underpants shifted and I could feel the warm, bloody wad of toilet paper fall down my pant leg and onto the floor. It seemed to happen in slow motion—just like in a movie when the heroine is about to experience an untimely and tragic death. One minute it was firmly in place and there was still the possibility of everything eventually working out okay. A few eternal seconds later Henry and I were staring at this bloody *thing* on the floor. It looked like maybe I'd given birth to a tiny, hairless white rabbit. *This cannot be happening to me*, I thought, my eyes and mouth open wide in horrified surprise. Henry and I made our moves at the same moment. But while Henry was merely curious, I was purely desperate, and desperation won. I grabbed up the bloody wad while Henry was still sniffing it, and hid it as best I could in my palm pressed against my side.

Just then two sophomores in a shoving match tripped over Henry, who let out a yelp. I dropped Rosalie's backpack (but held onto the bloody wad of toilet paper) and had this sudden crazy image of Henry attacking my crotch or the bloody toilet paper or both. I leaped backward and landed hard on somebody's foot, turned around to apologize, and looked straight into Doug Fulmer's dark brown eyes. I was so close to him I could smell him—an intoxicating mixture of peppermint, soap, and some kind of guy smell that always reminds me of wet dogs. I stumbled backward at the shock of being so close to him, and he grabbed my arm to steady me. I went weak in the knees.

Even though I'd fantasized fervently about Doug Fulmer for the last few months, I'd never spoken to him in real life. Now here he was sucking all the air from my lungs with a single glance, and all I could think to do was look down at the floor and make sure I wasn't dripping blood all over it like a dog in heat.

"Need some help?" he asked.

Those eyes! That smile! I didn't trust myself to answer because the irony of it all had finally hit me: the irony that my greatest hope—*Doug Fulmer talking to me!*— and my greatest fear—Doug Fulmer talking to me while I'm leaking bodily fluids, holding an embarrassing wad of bloody toilet paper, fending off the crotch-sniffing Henry while helping a blind girl on crutches make it to her next class without falling down a flight of stairs, not to mention worrying that I'll get caught cutting the rest of my classes and perhaps *not* be able to talk my way out of it (although, if you had asked me this morning, I never would have guessed *any* of this was my greatest fear)— were all twisted together in this one horrible moment.

And then, just when I thought it could not possibly get any worse, along came Melanie Fritchie, her black hair swinging, her too-perfect smile aimed at Doug.

Charm oozed out of her in his direction; I sensed only an icy disregard toward me. She pulled a sheet of notebook paper from her bag and handed it to me. "Hi, Doug . . . ," she cooed, stepping nearer to him than necessary and placing her hand on his arm. I gritted my teeth and glanced at this month's assignment: three hundred words, due next Wednesday, on the new garbage disposal system in the cafeteria kitchen. I sighed in grudging admiration at this new low in unpopular topics she'd managed to achieve. But I was relieved that I now had someplace to hide the bloody wad of toilet paper, and quickly wrapped it up out of view of the crowds in the hallway that were starting to gather around the two sophomores who had progressed from shoving to grappling.

Someone got pushed into Melanie, whose opened bag flew out of her hands and spewed its contents all over the floor in a three-foot arc radiating outward from her. Wallet, hairbrush, perfume, pens, markers, keys, tissues, lipsticks, mascara, a red lace bra, and best of all—closest to me and farthest from her—a tampon. She made a small, strangled noise, which I recognized as embarrassment. We both dropped to a squat, Melanie grabbing for the bra and me grabbing for the tampon, which I tucked in my pocket. She mouthed the words *Thank you*, which confused me for a second, since I had just stolen a tampon from her.

Then Doug went over to either join the spectators or break up the fight, I couldn't tell which, and I finally realized what Melanie's "thank you" was for—I'd saved her the embarrassment of having her tampon on public display there in the hallway.

An idea formed as I mechanically continued to help pick up her belongings and shove them back in her purse. Even though I was so wet I wanted to run to the nearest girls' room with the prized tampon, I was more determined to turn this horrible morning around. Melanie felt indebted to me now, and I was beginning to see how I could make this work in my favor. I took a deep breath and steeled myself.

Doug had separated the squabbling sophomores in a flash and had come back to see if Melanie was okay. Melanie and I were just standing up again as I launched into my plan.

"Oh, Melanie, I think that's a great idea," I said to Melanie's uncomprehending face. "Melanie wants me to do a series of feature articles on the unsung athletes, Doug. She thinks I should start with you."

Melanie's head snapped back as if I'd thrown ice water at her. Doug's face brightened. "Hey, great idea, Melanie! Other editors acted like soccer players didn't even exist." Melanie mumbled something in response, but Doug was looking at me, so I wasn't paying her much attention. "What's your name, reporter?" he asked me.

"Carly Pender," I told him. "Maybe over the weekend we can get together for that interview." The first of many, I hoped. A really good article would probably require a series of very long interviews. . . .

"I have a game tomorrow," he said.

"I'll be there," I told him. "We can talk afterward."

"Great!" he said. "See you then."

I gave him a smile that I hoped would sear itself into his memory, then suddenly remembered Rose and Henry. They were nowhere to be seen. I guess they'd managed without my help after all. I walked away in what I prayed didn't look like the mad rush to the girls' room it actually was.

In the girls' room at last, I cleaned up as best I could, gathered up my belongings and headed toward the exit for the long walk home. It had been a rather horrible morning, but the fact that I had a date with Doug Fulmer after the game tomorrow (in a literal if not romantic sense) more than made up for it. And even though there was that mind-numbing assignment about the garbage disposal system still ahead, at least I'd wheedled my way into writing one feature article.

The brisk walk calmed me and pushed the tension from my body. I was enjoying the fresh November air when I suddenly realized I didn't know what had happened to the wad of bloody toilet paper. I couldn't remember throwing it away. I hadn't panicked and shoved it in my pocket or backpack. I was sure I hadn't dropped it on the floor. What had I done with it?

My mind wandered back through the morning, and with a gasp I realized what had happened. I was now twice as glad I wouldn't be in school the rest of the day. Because I realized that the next time Melanie Fritchie went through her purse, she was in for a rather unpleasant surprise.

the heroic quest of
douglas mcgawain
by David Lubar

it was dark out. And stormy. No matter. We were warm and dry, and well cuddled. I was on the couch with Tracy, watching a movie down in her rec room. Rick and Debbie were with us, also well cuddled. Life was good. The night was young. If I were frozen in this moment for all of eternity, I'd be happy. And, as I said, well cuddled.

I'd only been going out with Tracy for two months, but I'd never met anyone who fit so well into every part of my life. Whether we were studying, dancing, driving, sharing a sundae, playing table tennis, walking in the park, hanging out, or cuddling, it felt right. We belonged together.

While the moment couldn't last forever, I expected it to at least last until we watched the movies we'd rented.

Then chivalry reared its ugly head.

Debbie drained the soda from her glass and shook it.

Rick, like any well-trained guy, responded to the clinking in the manner in which we'd all been conditioned. "I'll get it." He rose from his seat and carried the glass upstairs.

He returned a moment later, the glass still empty.

"Got any more diet Dr Pepper?" he asked Tracy.

"Just what was up in the fridge," she said. "I guess we're out."

I wasn't surprised. For all her charm, beauty, wit, and magnificence, for all that I adored her, I was well aware that Tracy had an insignificant flaw. She wasn't great at planning ahead. She tended to run out of things. For that very reason, I'd brought a twelve pack of Mountain Dew with me. I didn't mind. Her flaw offered me countless chances to play the hero.

"No big deal," Debbie said. "I can drink something else."

"There's plenty of Dew," I said.

Rick constructed an optical triangle, glancing from the glass to Debbie to some distant point beyond the wall in the general direction of the cold, wet world.

"I'll go for some," he said.

The triangle graduated to a quadrilateral as he

included me in his circuit. I loosened my grip on Tracy. There were rules for this sort of thing. My response was as ritually ordained as saying "Bless you" to a sneeze. I spoke the required phrase. "I'll go with you."

"You sure?" Rick asked, initiating the second round.

"Yup." End of ritual.

No big deal. We'd hop in the car. Drive to the nearest store. Grab some soda. Maybe some chips. And return as heroes. To be suitably rewarded with strokes and kisses for our bravery.

No big deal at all.

"Hang on," Tracy said as I walked toward the door.

This, too, was part of the ritual. She had a craving. Yet more chance for me to save the day with Cool Ranch Doritos, Twizzlers, or some other object to satisfy her desires. Instead of telling me what she wanted, she rooted through her purse. I waited patiently, pleased by an opportunity to be gallant.

Tracy frowned, shuffled through the contents a bit more, then shook her head, pulled out her wallet, and held out a ten-dollar bill. That was odd. I was more than happy to pay for her craving.

"Could you get me some tampons while you're out?"

An electrical storm danced through my brain as it tried to make sense of those words.

Oh my god.

Tampons?

Guys don't buy tampons. We just don't. Everybody knows that. "Uh . . . ?" I sorted through a thousand potential excuses. They all sucked. Besides, this wasn't some nameless damsel in distress. This was Tracy.

As I reached for the money, the chivalric code wrestled with unknown worlds. Under any other circumstance whatsoever, I was supposed to say, "That's okay. My treat."

But *tampons*? Does a guy pick up the tab?

Clueless, I took the money.

Tracy spoke. A brand. A variety. A box color. "Want to write it down?" she asked.

"I got it," I said, repeating the details to myself, knowing I could never allow the existence of hard evidence in the form of a written mention.

Rick was silent as we dashed through the rain to the car.

"You ever . . . ?" I asked when I got inside.

He shook his head. We drove to the Seven Eleven

which, despite its name, was open well past midnight. Rick went to the cooler. I scanned the aisles. There they were. A couple small boxes. I stared at them, trying to decipher the meanings of the words and compare them against the phrases Tracy had spoken. *Light, medium, heavy, super, extra, carefree, fancy,* and on and on like sacred words from the chanted mantra of a foreign cult.

"You ready?" Rick asked. He stood at the end of the aisle, holding the soda in a bag, obviously unwilling to move any closer.

A woman headed down the aisle. I shifted my attention away from the tampons and grabbed something else. Oh crap—hemorrhoid suppositories. I tossed the box back on the shelf and snatched the first masculine thing I saw. Shaving cream. "Hey," I called to Rick. "Look. This one's extra rich for dealing with manly stubble." I rubbed my cheek and tried to appear deep in thought.

The woman stared at me for an instant, then grabbed a bottle of Tylenol and moved on.

I sighed and studied the boxes again.

"Just pick one," Rick said. "What's the difference?"

I shook my head. Tracy had entrusted me. I wasn't

going to fail. She'd always been there when I needed her.

"Let's go to Shop Rite," I said.

We drove onto Rt. 309 to the Shop Rite in the strip mall. As we pulled into the lot, I could see it was closed.

But past the rows of shut stores, at the far end, I spotted salvation. "Big Wayne's is open," I said. It was a discount warehouse. Dad had gotten us a family membership. I didn't go there much, except when I wanted to load up on school supplies or huge quantities of frozen burritos.

Rick pulled to the curb by Big Wayne's. "I'll wait here," he said.

Bastard. But I couldn't blame him. I wouldn't want to be anywhere near a guy buying tampons either.

"Right back." I got out of the car and went in, praying to the great Earth Mother that Big Wayne's would have tampons.

Oh man, did they have tampons.

A whole freaking aisle. Boxes in every color. Boxes in every brand. Boxes in every length, width, and voltage for all I knew. But every single one of the boxes was about half the size of a full-grown bull elephant.

Damn. There was no way I could pretend to study

shaving cream. Anyone facing these shelves was after only one thing. At least the aisle was empty of other shoppers for the moment.

I found the section with Tracy's brand. But that was just the beginning. Good lord. There were so many varieties, I started to question my own limited grasp of female anatomy. It couldn't be this complicated.

There. Up at the top. Blue boxes. She'd said blue. And the words matched those she'd spoken. I'd found them.

Eight feet off the floor.

I jumped and tried to grab a box.

I was barely able to bump it with my fingers. I looked around for a ladder. Nothing in sight. I jumped again and managed to prod the box slightly from the shelf. Four more jumps and I got it jutting out far enough that I could knock it free.

Along with about twenty other boxes.

Thanks to a panicked leap backward, I avoided being killed by the sharp corner of a box holding hundreds of tampons. Wouldn't that make a great headline?

But I had what I needed.

I've always cleaned up my own messes. Until now. I left the aisle, and the pile of boxes. The twinge of guilt was a nice break from the stew of embarrassment, shame, fear, and confusion I'd been steeping in since I'd left the house.

Now, one final obstacle.

I approached the registers. Three were open. I checked my cashier options. A teen girl. No way. An older woman. Maybe in her late thirties. Bright blond hair. Long red nails. Very sexy body. The kind of woman who could make me feel like a little boy, or cut me in half with a sneer. Nope. Last choice. An old guy. Yeah.

As I headed for him, he flicked off the light above the register. I took a chance and plopped down the box.

"Closed," he said.

I implored him with my eyes. I pointed at the box. I sent a mental message, from one guy to another. *I'm buying tampons, for God's sake. Help me out.* It was no use.

I carried the box to the short line at the blond woman's register. Too late, I noticed that there were a couple guys right in front of me dressed like they'd just finished a shift at a mill.

One glanced over his shoulder, started to look away, then stared at the box in my hands. He nudged his buddy. They both looked back and laughed.

I could feel myself shrinking to a size small enough to hide behind the box.

God. I realized people were staring at me from all over.

Finally the guys in front of me were done. One blew me a kiss as he left. I put the box on the conveyor.

The woman—her name tag said Myrna—scanned the box without even glancing at me. I handed her the money. She gave me my change and a receipt. No bag. Big Wayne's didn't believe in frills like bags.

I couldn't believe I was going to escape without one final knife thrust.

Then she spoke.

"Girlfriend?"

I looked up as I grabbed the box.

"Yeah."

"Good for you, sugar." Myrna gave me a tired smile. "Takes a real man to buy tampons for a lady."

"Thanks."

As I walked off, she called, "You ever break up, you come see me. I could use a real man."

Whoa. The fantasy that danced through my mind was quickly extinguished by the knowledge that, whether I was a real man or not, I already had a real woman. And she was waiting for me. Still, I was walking a bit taller when I left the store, until the wind hit me in the face.

As I hunched over and rushed through the rain to Rick's car, I imagined the damage that would occur if the box got wet. I could see it swell to even more immense proportions, then explode, showering me in tampons.

"Christ, put that in the trunk," Rick said when I started to get inside. "If it will fit. You planning to supply the whole field hockey team?"

"Lighten up. They don't bite."

He popped the trunk and I put the tampons away.

"Can we go now?" Rick asked.

"Absolutely."

"Good." He pulled away from the curb. "I'm done for the night. No more errands."

"That's for sure." I glanced at the trunk, hoping I hadn't somehow screwed up and bought the wrong thing. Outside, the rain fell even harder against the windshield.

When we got back, I handed Tracy the box. "They didn't have anything smaller," I said. "I hope this is okay."

"You did great." She rewarded me with a smile. "Thanks. Sorry to make you run out in the rain."

"No problem," I said. "No problem at all."

"My hero," Tracy said.

"Hey, whose hero am I?" Rick asked as he handed Debbie a can of soda.

Debbie frowned at the can and then at Rick. "This isn't diet."

I cuddled down on the couch with Tracy.

"Guess I'll go get some more soda," Rick said. He glanced at me. "Yeah . . . I'll go out again. . . ."

"Hurry back," I said. Then I turned my full attention to cuddling with my lady.

moon time child
by Alice McGill

it *is Saturday, the third day of April and nighttime in the cabin.* I am Salome. Blind Eller, the old quilting woman, is asleep at long last. This morning the auctioneer struck me off to this Grey Plantation. "A strong and healthy breeder—seven hundred and fifty dollars—SOLD!" he bellowed.

"They must think you a good breeder," Blind Eller said from one of the overstuffed cots as soon as I stepped through her cabin door. "You tall and thick, and young," she said like she could see me. I answered not a word. I wondered how she lost her sight.

"You ready for to be a breeder?" she asked. Again, silence on my part. Despite that I am three months into my thirteenth year of living, there has been no monthly flow.

Her forehead frowned but her sealed eyelids marked her face like straight lines.

I wish she had asked me about the Smyth Plantation, where I am from. Before the auction I was playmate and companion to young Anna Smyth. We were the same year's children—born in 1839. We slept in the same room; my bed was as big as hers. We ate from the same table and wore matching frocks at Anna's say-so, like twins. When Miss Huntington came to teach book reading and ciphering, I learned alongside my friend Anna. What grand times we had waltzing in the ballroom and riding ponies. Then Anna sickened and died.

Three days after the funeral, Miss Billie, Anna's mother, could not bear my presence in the household. Anna's daddy, Mister George, watched his wife send me to reside in the quarters. My bundle of a few frocks, writing books, ink and quill was thrown after me into a filthy cabin—from there to the slave auction. Before I was to step up on the block, Miss Billie yanked away my few valuables one by one until I cried out so loudly. Not knowing the contents of the bag, the auctioneer quickly low-voiced a few words to her, and she threw back my little bag of writing things. The overseer thought it would be difficult to sell an unhappy slave.

Still, Miss Billie hissed in my ear, after signing the

bill of sale, "If you are caught writing they will send you as far as wind and water can carry you, and I shall be the gladder for it. You should have died—not my Anna!" So here I am. To show that all I had is not gone, I must write. Someday a young girl may find my writings tucked away in the hidey holes of this cabin. I pray that she can read. I must pinch the candle. Good night.

fourth day of april, morning in the cabin

Today is Sunday. Fields of workers left singing on their way to the spring planting. Blind Eller is eating vittles I brought to her from the cook's hand at the back door of the master's house. I have not seen him. Missus Grey came to the door and smiled at me like Miss Billie. She said I was to take care of Blind Eller in the cabin and lead her to the quilting room. Once there, I must thread her needles, cut quilting squares from end bolts of cloth, and wham cotton to make soft batting for quilt linings. I have never beaten cotton before.

Blind Eller keeps turning her head toward my scratching pen. A little smile is playing around her lips as she nods her head to the sound. I think she knows I am writing. Something tells me I can trust her not to tell.

"Did you see your moon time yet, child?" She faced me with this question like she could see inside my heart.

"Moon time?" I asked, not knowing.

"Your monthly issue what come every time 'cording to the slice of the moon," she said, still facing me.

"No, ma'am," said I. Now that I think of it, moon time is a better way of speaking of this strange business—like a secret only best friends should know about each other. Anna reached her moon time two months before she died.

The old quilting woman is chewing on a meat skin and sopping the last bit of greasy molasses from her bowl. She just asked if I had spoken to any young girls who live in the next few cabins. I told her I had seen some of them on my way to get vittles. Two of them giggled like they knew something about me I did not know. I refused to greet them. One of the gigglers snarled behind my back, "She b'having like Miss Better Off." Sweat ran down my face. Blind Eller said no more. I am afraid to ask her about the two that had big stomachs. I do not want a big stomach. I am sweating again. I must help Blind Eller tidy herself.

●

sixth day of april, nighttime in the cabin

My hands are sore from cutting squares and whamming cotton. The quilting frame slipped off the hook two times. My head wrap fell off without my knowing. Now my hair is covered with cotton fuzz. Blind Eller and I spent nine hours in the quilting room. I told her how easily Miss Billie taught me and Anna how to make embroidered samplers that said,

> Anna & Salome Smyth are our names &
> with our needles we wrought the same, 1849.

Miss Billie made so much over our fine stitching to her friends.

Blind Eller sucked her teeth and cackled out that I was a companion or pet for true but still a slave in the Smyth household. Says she, "I could tell they musta learned you something 'cause you talk too good not to have learning. You be careful 'bout scratching down on paper." She will not report that I can read and write. I wonder if she knows that I have been hiding my writing things under a floorboard.

•

ninth day of april, morning in the cabin

Missus Grey just left the cabin. "I have a fine crop of babies coming along, Salome," she said with her eyes fixed on me like a chicken hawk. "This Saturday night, I'll give you a pass to go with the girls to the bounce down in the bottom," says she, sweeping her long skirt out the door.

Blind Eller said a bounce is fiddling and dancing with strong, healthy young men from other plantations. "You ain't got to worry 'bout nothing 'cause you ain't reached your moon time," she said. Still I do not wish to attend. I pray that I never reach my moon time. Blind Eller says Missus Grey would not like it if I did not go bouncing or whatever the dance. Today is Friday.

ninth day of april at night

I must write even though Blind Eller is watching me with disapproving ears. "You be careful," she just said. I told her my body is not to bounce in the bottom. Well, let her stew. Eppy, one of the girls with a big stomach, stopped by to choose her quilt today. I did not know that new mothers are to receive new quilts after the babies are born. If the poor soul births twins, then two quilts are given. Missus Grey's words, "a nice crop of babies," come to mind—sounds like she was talking about something growing out of the dirt. I do not remember having a mother. Was she a breeder too? I need her. Oh, how I do need her. I am ashamed for not thinking of her before.

Blind Eller just asked, "You ever feel a cramp in your stomach? How old you be? Missus Grey know you ain't reached your moon time? If not," says she, "you tell Missus. Then we think on it some. Be careful." My heart aches. Have I been working on a quilt for myself? There is no one to help me but Blind Eller, and she is so full of questions. Where are the answers to the questions I am afraid to ask?

tenth day of april at night

This morning I told Missus Grey I had not reached my moon time. She stormed through the cabin door. "My bill of sale says 'breeder' and never been busted," she snapped. She ordered me to stand up so she could dig her fingers around my waist and demand, "Did some scrawny, unhealthy buck bust you?"

"Bust me?" I asked like a dumb mule. Blind Eller

spoke up and told her I had never been with a man because I didn't even know what busted meant. That satisfied Missus Grey. She departed, saying I should not go to the bounce.

Anna and I did talk on about where babies came from—out of the woman's stomach. We never did talk about how the baby got inside the stomach. I think I know. Anna and I used to sneak to the stable and watch the horses. After a while a little foal was born.

Miss Billie would have gone into conniptions if she had known how we laughed at her sister's bulging stomach. That was Miss Sally. She came to stay with us so her husband would not see the ugliness of carrying a baby. Her baby was born in the room next to Miss Billie's.

eleventh day of april in the morning

My mind is racing. Missus Grey was in the cabin when I returned with vittles. She left quickly with my not knowing what had been discussed.

Last night Anna came to my dreams. We were running through a field of yellow flowers, swinging matching baskets of fresh pears.

Five breeders—I don't want to know their names—just passed by the cabin whispering and laughing about last night's bouncing dance. The old woman is eating quietly and slowly, like she is thinking about something that she is not going to tell me. Now she is smiling and nodding her head. I must comb and plait her hair today.

The rows of field-workers' cabins are filled with laughter and playing children. The overseer rationed out their week's supply of cornmeal, pork skins, jugs of molasses, and dried beans and peas.

Blind Eller is still quiet. I so dislike the task of calling upon enough nerve to question her about her talk with Missus Grey. I wish she could see me.

fourteenth day of april at night

More end bolts of cloth came in today. We spent ten hours in the quilting room. All of the quilt toppings resemble a mishmash of red, blue, and yellow colors trimmed in blue.

No mention of the conversation with Missus Grey. For the past few days, every now and again, Blind Eller burst into humming a song.

•

fifteenth day of april at night

I am tired. Blind Eller is asleep. She told me she was once a baby catcher for breeders. I am sorry I asked how she caught babies, for she pulled her frock up around her waist, showing her undergarment, and spread her old legs and said, "Baby came from here, head first. I caught him coming out." She said that would learn me to know I am not where I was. I almost spit up my supper. I am afraid to look at the moon.

seventeenth day of april in the morning

I found a small cloth bag of crushed leaves under Blind Eller's pillow. She asked, "Well, what you think of it?" There was a sweet mint smell. "What is it?" I asked, pulling the drawstring open. The old woman said it was a potion to make cold tea for me to drink. Then my moon time would come down. I cried out. "Stop that," Blind Eller said. She told me I was not to tell Missus Grey that I had not drunk tea.

I sprinkled about a tablespoon of the dried leaves in her hand like she asked. "Don't ever tell nary a soul or I will lose more than my eyes," she said, and rubbed her hands together. Crumbly bits and pieces fell on the floor. The cabin has a sour mint odor. Maybe this tea is what Missus Grey talked about to Blind Eller earlier this week. The old woman is humming her tune.

twentieth day of april in the morning

This is the fourth day I have sprinkled tea leaves into Blind Eller's hand. Missus Grey just left with a smile on her face. She thinks I am happy because I smiled at her. Last night Blind Eller hugged me like a dear friend. That's why I am happy. I am ready to wham the batting and cut the squares. Blind Eller is true. Good night.

twenty-first day of april at night

Eppy screams every five minutes. It is time for someone to catch her baby. "Naw, naw, I can't!" she keeps screaming. Blind Eller is leaning her ear in the direction of the screams, two cabins down from ours. She said the catching woman is too old to know what to do for Eppy. Missus Grey is shouting, "Eppy, if you don't stop such fuss, I will send for Doctor Swenson to come here and cut that baby out of you." I know Missus Grey is lying because Eppy would die.

•

twenty-fourth day of april at night

Eppy's eight pound boy baby is blossoming. The poor girl could hardly walk, but she was smiling when she came to receive her new quilt this morning. I folded her quilt and tied twine around it for her. The baby catcher will stay with her for a few more days. Then Eppy will have to go back to work in the weaving room and take her baby with her. Please, Blind Eller, do not let me earn a new quilt. If I said I hated Miss Billie and Missus Grey before, now I hate them even more. Good night.

twenty-ninth day of april in the morning

Feels like a hundred frogs are leaping over each other in the bottom of my stomach. Please let me spit up my breakfast so it will go away forever. I am too scared to let Blind Eller know. Did she not destroy the tea leaves? Is it the scent of the tea leaves that's causing my stomach to cramp? My moon time will be the death of my spirit. Oh, Anna, why did you die instead of me? You are somewhere singing of lavender blue and highland laddie songs. Here I am in hell, and it is not my fault.

•

twenty-ninth day of april at night

No blood flow. The cramp left on its own. I told Blind Eller. It surprised me that she laughed heartily upon hearing about how much I hated Miss Billie and Missus Grey for my suffering. "What hate gonna do for you?" she asked. "It makes me feel better," says I. "Hate will take away your good sense," she said. Not possible, I am thinking. She sang.

> If you don't b'lieve I've been redeemed
> take me to the water,
> follow me down to Jordan's stream
> take me to the water
> to be baptized.

I joined her thin high voice as best I could. Now my stomach is quiet.

fourth day of may at night

The moon is full. Leaping frogs returned. Wetness feels sticky. I cannot look, but I know there is blood. Oh, my God, my moon time is here. I told Blind Eller. She hugged me and said, "You womanish now."

The folded pieces of white cloth on the foot of my cot are there for me. How did the old woman know to place them without my seeing? Why is she smiling like an old cat? Is this what she discussed with Missus Grey too? Has she tricked me somehow? I don't know whether or not hate has taken over my good sense, but something has done so. I hate that I am womanish too.

fifth day of may, morning in the cabin

My stomach is cramping. Missus Grey just left the cabin. She gave orders for me to help with stitching quilts. Three more girls are expecting babies. She bragged on Eppy's boy. Blind Eller smiled and praised this woman's good fortune.

sixth day of may at night in the cabin

Today I stitched quilts as fast as I could but could not keep up with Blind Eller. Her fingers glide from one end of the frame to the other without rest.

Well, my first moon time is over. I wanted to, somehow, burn my used cloths. Blind Eller said the old folks told her that would be like burning up my life. So I dug a hole behind the quilting room and buried my moon time. Blind Eller said we must tell Missus Grey. The good old woman is right. Eventually someone will surely see me burying my secret. Yesterday I saw breeders dropping their used cloths in pots of boiling lye water. Then they rinsed until the whiteness returned. A clothesline for drying is situated in the back of the cabins.

eighth day of may in the morning

Blind Eller jumped when I told her word was whispered at the kitchen door that Master Grey is down with sickness. Doctor Swenson is by his side night and day. I think little of his good or poor health. I have caught sight of him in the kitchen but twice since coming here. The good old woman is rocking back and forth. I must hug her and plait her hair.

tenth day of may at night in the cabin

This morning before dawn, clapping bells aroused the plantation. Master Grey is dead. Not a soul worked the whole day. At three o'clock, the slaves were called to pay their last respects to the master. "I cannot go," Blind

Eller said to me. "You look at him like my eyes."

Upon my return, she sat upon me with questions, and I answered to tell her Missus Grey shed a few tears as we passed the dark wood coffin. A few family friends stood aside and stared at us. None of us cried. Crepe covered the front door. The parlor windows were draped in black velvet. Master Grey's dark brown hair made his face appear as white as the wreaths of lilac flowers that hung on the parlor walls. His pale fingers clutched a Holy Bible.

Afterward she groaned a few times and said like she had made sure with, "Master Grey is dead and gone. He took away my sight 'cause I hid a helpless child's moon time. But I am still here—helping all I can." Blind Eller is not afraid. By the hum of a new tune, I know she will never tell me the details of her suffering. The moon time child she helped will be her forever secret. Now I am a moon time child. Now I see her almighty courage.

Until now my eyes were closed to everything except my fears, my anger, and my hatred. I am no better off than the rest of the breeders whom I have scorned because they laugh and giggle like they are happy. Now I know how they must be crying inside because they are treated like horses just like me. Even though I can read and write, I am no better off.

I had a good time living for a while, and I am glad of that. But if Anna had lived, where would I be after she had outgrown our matching games? What if she had taken a husband? I know the answers.

She would have found an obedient handmaid in me and a nurse to her children, but I would have been a slave for the rest of my life. I would have been expected to have children to nurse her children's children.

twelfth day of may at night

Blind Eller is under the covers. I have propped myself against her cot to write and talk. She agrees that I should tell Missus Grey about my moon time so I can attend the next bounce. The good old woman said that I should sit on the bench at the bounce and sing "Take me to the water," and a young man will find me. She said I am to do exactly as the young man says.

"What will the young man say?" I asked.

"In due time you will know," she answered. "I can help you better with no more than a spoonful of hush-hush at a time. The rest will be in your hands soon enough." With that said, she patted my shoulder until sleep overtook her.

The rest will be up to me. I must take charge of myself. Well, I will not be busted by any man even if I am womanish.

thirteenth day of may in the morning

I told Missus Grey my moon time had come and gone some days ago. Instantly she spurted lambasting words at me for not telling her the first day I saw blood. With tears in my eyes, I told her the master's sickness and death made me not want to bother her. She accepted this reason, dressed in widow's weeds but not showing any grief over her husband that I could see. Instead, her eyes filled with greed as she said, "You shall receive something pretty to wear to the bounce."

So now I expect to wear something better than my present shabby homespun. She expects a new baby.

fifteenth day of may in the morning

The sun is shining. Roxie and Monimya were surprised that I talked to them on my way to get vittles. Roxie has reached her fifteenth birthday. Monimya is thirteen like me. They are attending the bounce too. We do not work today.

My pretty something has arrived—one of Missus Grey's tired-looking frocks—but it is clean and has a petticoat too. She has sent word that at sundown, a wagonload of us will travel about a mile away to the bottom.

At least ten times Blind Eller reminded me of the song. She smiles every time I sing, "Take me to the water, take me to the water to be baptized."

The rest is up to me.

fifteenth day of may late at night

I am back in the cabin. The good old woman is smiling and laughing. I told her about how I bided my time to look around a bit. I found the bottom to be a shallow pit a little bigger than the Smyth's ballroom. Dancing feet have beaten the surface into hard clay. No benches but bales of hay scattered here and there. Young men stood on one side and the girls on the other, looking at one another. The overseer watched three fiddlers and two drummers assemble themselves in lantern light. I sat down and began to sing,

If you don't believe I've been redeemed
take me to the water,
Follow me down to Jordan's stream
take me to the water. . . .

The girls' side gaped at me like one big eye. Derisive laughter broke out on the male side. Then two young men, one behind the other, swaggered toward me. The one in front announced, "I take her—I don't care if she crazy." The other turned back, saying, "Help yoself."

Each nervous, giggling girl wondered which young man would choose to dance with her.

"Salome, I choose you. My name Jack," the young man said to me. This is the one, I thought to myself. What will he say next? "I give your name to da overseer," he said. Then he instructed me to give his name to Missus Grey. "Why?" I asked. He shook his head.

Suddenly drumming and fiddling urged dancers to jump into the bottom and keep their feet and hind parts to perfect rhythm. Jack grabbed my hand and we jumped into the bottom. I could hardly follow his dancing feet and catch my breath at the same time. Drums told my heart when to beat and when to stop beating. The fiddle strings gave a sad and a happy reply to every set of drumbeats. I cannot explain it. Never have I been in the midst of such music. My feet were moving to the beat. Monimya offered to take me aside to teach me how to dance better. I thought I was already dancing better than anyone at the bounce. Blind Eller laughed.

Blind Eller said all breeders must give the name of the young man that chose them to Missus Grey. I am tired but I am not sleepy.

sixteenth day of may, morning in the cabin

I told Jack's name to Missus Grey. She was so overjoyed in her widow's weeds. I suppose she knows he is healthy. No matter. I am in charge of myself. Thank goodness she cannot see that I am.

nineteenth day of may in the morning

Jack is to visit me in a cabin tonight, Missus Grey said. It seems that all seven breeders will spend the night in several makeshift cabins, not far from the bottom. We will be delivered there by wagon at sundown. I told Blind Eller. She is quiet.

nineteenth day of may before sundown

The sun is going down. The good old woman just gave me another spoonful of hush-hush. It sounded more like a whole bowlful.

Jack is her grandson. He is nineteen years old, a slave on the Fuller Plantation. His mother and father were sold away from there when he was ten years old. Blind Eller was a slave on the Fuller Plantation until she became a hired-out baby catcher for the Grey Plantation. But Master Grey was forced to buy her after he took her sight away.

I am to sing the song so Jack can find me quickly. He is taking me ten miles away to the Tar River. A boat will be waiting for us. I am crying. Blind Eller keeps telling me to stop. I do not know how to stop crying.

She tells me the happiness she feels is like seeing the sun shining. Her grandson, the last in her family, will have a chance at book learning and freedom at the same time. "You show him how. He look on you like the young lady you used to see at the Smyth place," she said. I know she means he will not take advantage of me. I believe her.

In a few years I will no longer be womanish but a

grown woman, still in charge of myself. I know this is as true as Blind Eller, the only true friend I have ever known. After I tear off these three pages to hide, no more paper will be left in my writing book. I will bury the ink and quill.

Blind Eller knows about my hidey-holes. Maybe she will tell a young girl about me. Maybe slavery will end. Maybe I will see Blind Eller again. The sun is going down. I just wrapped my arms around her neck. She is smiling. I hear the wagon coming across the field. I am ready to sing again because I am no longer a moon time child. If you are reading my writings, I thank you with all of my heart. Good evening.

the women's house

by Dianne Ochiltree

sparrow-Song's moccasins swished through fallen leaves as she searched for more acorns to place into her gathering basket. She loved to wander these paths, to wander off these paths, to climb the rocks and watch the broad river below, flowing on its way to the village far downstream. It was here that she most truly felt her kinship with all living things, and with her own true spirit.

She glided into a grove of ancient oak trees. This was her favorite spot, a secret meeting place that she and her friend Painted-Turtle had shared ever since they were old enough to explore the woodlands together. Perhaps she'd see him here today.

Pushing back feathery ferns, she spotted not acorns, but a jagged piece of flint on the forest floor. Instinctively she picked it up. It reminded her of another secret she shared only with Painted-Turtle.

Although female and therefore forbidden to make an arrowhead, Sparrow-Song had always been skilled at finding just the right stone for the task—far better than any of the boys her age, including Painted-Turtle, to whom she always gave the prized piece for his practice with the hammer stone. How *did* she know, she wondered, which pieces could be shaped easily, yet stay strong in use? It was as if the rock itself could speak to her somehow.

Sparrow-Song's thoughts were broken, sharp as the snap of a twig, by shouts from nearby. The happy sounds led her to a broad and rocky stretch of the riverbank. There stood Painted-Turtle, along with a small band of younger boys from the village.

"Perfect timing, Sparrow-Song," he called out as she approached them. "I was just about to show these tadpoles which rocks are best for weapon-making."

"You mean something like this?" asked Sparrow-Song, in mock innocence, offering him the piece of flint still in her hand.

"Why, yes, a perfect example," he told her with a wink. "You've made a lucky guess with this one."

"Lucky guess, eh?" Sparrow-Song teased. "Maybe

so . . . but there's no need to guess which one of us could better skip this stone across the river's surface. It's *me*," she said boldly.

"Is that a challenge?" asked Painted-Turtle, grinning. "The best of ten tries?"

"Yes, yes!" cried the younger boys in chorus, happy for a diversion from their rock-hunting chores. "A stone-skipping contest!"

As she tossed out the first stone, Sparrow-Song's stiff deerskin shirt pulled tightly across her chest. She winced as it skimmed her small breasts, realizing that she was still unaccustomed to having breasts at all, and that soon she would need to remake her shirt to accommodate their growing size. Why couldn't her breasts have chosen to appear in the summer, when there was no need for shirts at all?

In spite of this distraction, Sparrow-Song easily skipped stone after stone farther and faster than Painted-Turtle's. As the seventh round was about to begin, Sparrow-Song heard her mother in the distance, calling her name. She halted the contest abruptly.

"I've won this one anyway," she announced to the disappointed little boys. She brushed her hand against

Painted-Turtle's as she turned to go, and said, "Perhaps I'll allow you a rematch tomorrow."

Then Sparrow-Song raced away, following the trail of her mother's voice as it echoed in the cool morning air. She found her in the oak thicket, hands on her hips and a scowl on her face, with Sparrow-Song's two older sisters in tow.

"Where have you been, little daughter?" Rabbit-Woman demanded. "Did you not know the worry and fear in my heart when I could not find you? And what of your bold disobedience? You were supposed to stay in Sunrise Woods, looking for acorns."

"Look! There are two acorns hiding under Sparrow-Song's shirt," her oldest sister, Half-Moon, hooted. "I can see it won't be long before Sparrow-Song takes her first trip to the Women's House!" Her other sister, Touching-Leaf, giggled at the mocking remark. Sparrow-Song's face turned bright crimson.

Rabbit-Woman shook a finger in Half-Moon's face. "Silence, first daughter," she commanded. "Perhaps you do not have enough work to do? When hands are idle, foolish tongues flap." Rabbit-Woman thrust her own gathering basket into Half-Moon's free hand. "So, you will keep yourself busy by gathering even more acorns on your way back to the village." Rabbit-Woman shot a scornful look in Touching-Leaf's direction. "You, too, second daughter. Your basket can hold many more acorns. Now, go!"

Rabbit-Woman then turned her attention to Sparrow-Song. "Wandering off alone with Painted-Turtle is no longer proper behavior, little daughter," she scolded. "After all, you're nearly a woman now."

"You don't have to remind me!" exclaimed Sparrow-Song, who sat on a flat rock, arms folded tight across her chest.

Rabbit-Woman settled herself next to her silent daughter. "Perhaps Half-Moon spoke harshly as a crow," she told her, "but the words she spoke are true. Soon your monthly visits to the Women's House will begin. We have talked about this matter many times. You know exactly what to do."

Sparrow-Song blinked back angry tears. "No, I don't," she blurted. "I don't know anything about walking the path of a woman. I'm not ready!"

When she looked upon Sparrow-Song's troubled face, Rabbit Woman's own face softened. She said, in a gentler voice, "You cannot stop the change of the seasons, or the rising and setting of the sun. So it is with your first woman's blood." Sparrow-Song allowed her mother to encircle her in an embrace. "Don't be afraid—you will not walk your path alone," her mother whispered. The two sat, not speaking, for a time.

"Come now, little daughter," Rabbit Woman said at last. "Let's take up your things and go home." As she peered into Sparrow-Song's gathering basket, she asked, "What is this, that you've tucked alongside the acorns?"

"In truth, I don't know the name of the plant, or why I pulled it from the ground," Sparrow-Song admitted. "It just looked as if . . . as if it *wanted* me to pick it." Tears again welled in her eyes. "I suppose you're going to tell me I've done something else wrong!"

"No, no," replied Rabbit-Woman in a reassuring manner. "You've acted wisely to collect this plant, the black cohosh. Its root is helpful for women's pains and other troubles. Corn-Stalk told me, only yesterday, that she wished to add more to her supply."

"I will take it to her as soon as we return to the village," promised Sparrow-Song. She was pleased to have an errand that would keep her away from the wigwam, and her two cross sisters, for at least a few more moments today.

Because their home was near the village's most-used trail, Sparrow-Song's family often received news and visitors first. So it was today, when she saw her father returning—days early—from a hunting trip. Her mother and sisters bolted out of the wigwam at the sound of her cry, and now all four women surrounded Red-Hawk.

"What's wrong, Father?" gasped Sparrow-Song, her throat tight with fear. "Has someone been hurt? Was there an accident?"

"An accident, yes," Red-Hawk answered in a calming tone, "but not one of our men." He waved his hand toward a dozen or so braves approaching from the village trail. "We discovered them, a hunting party of men from the stony country, huddled under a sheltering rock near Big Deer Meadow. They had lost their way trying to return an injured hunter to their village," Red-Hawk explained. "Ah, here he comes now!"

Clinging unsteadily to Half-Moon's husband, Winter-Sky, was an older man, a wild-eyed stranger. His foot was swollen and wrapped in many soiled strips of leather.

Half-Moon rushed forward with grateful tears. She began to remove the hunting bow from Winter-Sky's back.

"Don't let her do that!" the stranger croaked into Winter-Sky's ear. "Unless you, too, want bad luck!"

Half-Moon's eyes flashed angrily. "I only intended to relieve my husband of *one* of his burdens!" she snapped. "Besides, what business is it of yours?"

"Sister, we must show our guest proper politeness, no matter what," Sparrow-Song hissed through clenched teeth. Half-Moon cast a dark look, but held her tongue.

"He says his wife has brought bad luck upon his hunting for many months now, to prove him a poor provider," Winter-Sky explained with a shrug, "so she will have just cause to divorce him."

Sparrow-Song stared at the stranger in disbelief.

"It's true!" he argued. "Again no game to bring home. It's all her fault! My wife waits, too long, to leave our wigwam for the Women's House. She touches my bow and arrows on her way there, every month . . . my fishing hooks, too. And see now, the latest result? My own weapon wounds me!" The young braves looked down at their moccasins in embarrassed silence.

Sparrow-Song touched a hand to the man's forehead. "Perhaps his fever causes him to speak foolishly. We should give our guest your cup of tea," Sparrow-Song told Touching-Leaf. She snatched the wooden cup from Touching-Leaf's hand and pressed it into the stranger's.

"But I need it more than he does!" Touching-Leaf complained.

"And *he* doesn't have cramps," protested Half-Moon. "He just has bad luck!"

"This bark tea helps a fever, too," Sparrow-Song shot back at them both.

"*You* will make me another cup, then," whined Touching-Leaf.

"Besides, can't bad hunting luck be caused by other things?" asked Half-Moon with a smug look.

"Yes, perhaps this man hasn't made proper sacrifices to the Keeper of the Game or other spirits," admitted Red-Hawk.

"And don't forget, there are other shortcomings that could drive a woman to throw a husband's belongings outside her wigwam," added Rabbit-Woman, a twinkle in her eyes. "Although, husband, *I* have no cause for complaint." At this, Half-Moon, Touching-Leaf, and

Sparrow-Song suppressed smiles of amusement.

"There will be a feast tonight in the Long House, to give proper welcome to our visitors from the stony country," Red-Hawk said when he returned from the council meeting.

Touching-Leaf, who had been sulking, suddenly brightened. "A celebration, yes!" she exclaimed. "Did you see that handsome brave among them, the tall one with the snake tattoo on his cheek? Tonight I will make him forget all the girls in his village back home! I must select just the right beads and ear pendants to wear, and . . ."

"First, you must fetch smoked shad from the storage pit for me," corrected Rabbit-Woman. "We should start our cooking at once." Touching-Leaf pouted but obeyed her mother nonetheless.

Touching-Leaf's excitement over the celebration had caused a fresh worry to leap, swift as a frightened doe, into Sparrow-Song's heart. After her first visit to the Women's House, her time of courtship would begin. She would be introduced to suitors, until a match had been agreed upon by her family. What if her future husband was not one of the older boys from her own village, someone she already knew, but instead, a stranger from a neighboring land, like the brave whom Touching-Leaf hoped to charm tonight?

Half-Moon picked up a bone needle and sinew thread and began to repair a tear in Winter-Sky's best pair of buckskin leggings. Sparrow-Song sat next to her, pounding cornmeal for the fire-cakes she knew her mother would also wish to prepare for the feast.

"This will please Winter-Sky greatly." Half-Moon sighed as she squinted at her handiwork in progress. "He will look his finest tonight." She lowered her voice. "I am happy to welcome the young hunters . . . but why should we celebrate the arrival of that miserable old man? Unlucky, ha!"

"His injury confused him," admonished Sparrow-Song. "He meant you no offense." She rubbed her forehead and frowned as she thought again about the stranger's story. "The whole business isn't fair," she insisted. "Why must you, or I, or any other female be banished to the Women's House, just because it is said that even the *sight* of a menstruating woman brings bad luck upon the men of the village?"

"Because it is the way of things, little daughter,"

reminded Rabbit-Woman as she re-entered the wigwam for a cooking pot. Half-Moon and Sparrow-Song looked up in surprise. "Rabbits have large ears, and so do I," their mother said with a smile.

"Besides, going to the Women's House is not so bad," added Half-Moon. "You will see for yourself."

Sparrow-Song rubbed her forehead again. All the worry and thought about the Women's House rattling around in her head had caused it to ache. She decided to make herself a cup of bark tea, too.

That night the people filled the Long House with their many conversations, pressed so tightly together that the room buzzed like a beehive. But when Sun-Rider, their shaman, shook the sacred turtle-shell rattles, all fell silent. Taking a handful of cedar clippings, he sprinkled them over the center fire and blessed the gathering, sending up prayers on the sharp-scented smoke.

Their chief, Wind-in-Trees, next offered a lengthy welcoming speech. The eldest of the elders urged their guests to enjoy the tribe's hospitality, along with the bounty of the land-where-hills-gather, as long as they wished. Then, at last, everyone feasted on a mountain of food: whole roasted game birds, skewered venison, and stewed rabbit, along with many other delicacies simmering in clay pots. All except Sparrow-Song, that is.

"You've hardly eaten a thing!" Half-Moon chided. "Not even Mother's fire-cakes, your favorite!"

Touching-Leaf also saw Sparrow-Song's bowl still filled with food. "Sparrow-Song! If you don't eat something now, how will you have strength to dance late into the night, as you love to do?" she asked merrily, tossing her glossy black hair over her shoulder. This allowed her gaze to travel across the room and fall upon the handsome brave with the snake tattoo. "I heard someone call him Gray-Feather. And see how I have woven the feathers of a gray dove into my hair tonight? It's a good omen!"

Sparrow-Song felt as if the dull ache in her head had now fallen into her unsettled stomach. She did not answer Touching-Leaf's questions, but instead stared blankly at her sister, who chattered on without any encouragement. In truth, Sparrow-Song didn't know why the food on her plate did not jump into her mouth, as it usually did at a village feast. She'd spent most of her time enjoying the other pleasures of a celebration, such as watching the people and admiring the adornments they wore, beautiful things made from tooth and antler, claw and bone. Her eyes found Painted-Turtle now.

She noticed a new black amulet hung around Painted-Turtle's neck. He had also painted a blue stripe along one side of his face and gathered his hair—which usually hung loose around his shoulders—with a snakeskin at the back of his neck. It made him look older, she thought.

Half-Moon's eyes, too, darted across the room. She muttered, "I see my husband takes out his clay pipe to smoke with our visitors. I do not believe he will join us again for a long time. I must gather up his bowl and clean it outside." Once again she shook her head disapprovingly at Sparrow-Song. "Here, let me take yours, too. The village dogs will enjoy this, little sister, if you won't!"

As pipes were lit and dinners digested, the elders began to tell stories. These were far older than the storytellers themselves—ancient myths and legends of men and spirits, of demons and heroes, and of how things came to be in the world. At length an old woman strode forward to tell her tale. She held herself tall and erect, in spite of her weathered face and shock of snow-white hair.

"The first human being was a pregnant woman," Corn-Stalk intoned, "who was cast down from heaven. Just as the woman was about to fall into the Great Waters below, a sea turtle rose up, offering her a safe resting place upon its shell. The turtle brought with him much foam, which formed itself into land. Thus, the Earth rides a turtle, swimming upon the seas." Corn-Stalk clasped her gnarled hands together in front of her, knuckles up, so all could see.

"Soon after, the pregnant woman went into labor. She first bore a deer, a bear, and a wolf. She continued to give birth to many other creatures, until she had filled the world with living things . . . including two from whom we, the Original People, are descended."

Corn-Stalk now paused to look into the faces of her audience. Sparrow-Song was certain those sharp, black eyes could see into her very heart. "Through the labor of the Mother of the World, life was made possible," the ancient healer said at last. "My story has ended."

Although Sparrow-Song had heard this story many times, tonight—for the first time—she began to think that the woman's path, although difficult, was one of great worth to many. She vowed that *she* would never spend her time thinking of nothing but suitors or dressing her hair so thick with bear grease that it shone like a wet otter, as Touching-Leaf now did, so vain and proud. Or worse, spending day and night thinking of nothing but pleasing a husband, as Half-Moon now must.

Soon the celebration moved outside, to the village's common ground, where a bonfire now burned as bright as the midday sun. Away from their warming flames, the night breeze was cool. Many women tonight wore their finest mantles of turkey feathers or furs, sewn together. Half-Moon had an ornate one of rabbit and fox, and Sparrow-Song searched for it now in the crowd. But the smoke from the bonfire seemed to blur everything together, and she could not pick her out.

It was not difficult, however, to find Touching-Leaf, Sparrow-Song thought irritably. She looked sideways at her sister's face, brightly painted with fanciful designs. Sparrow-Song had decorated her face far more sensibly, with a small dot of red on each cheek, as had her mother.

Notes flowed out of a flute carved from the leg of a deer. Then came answering thumps from a drum of deerskin stretched over a water-filled log. The people gathered themselves around the bonfire, and with a chorus of chanting, the dancing began.

"Mother," begged Touching-Leaf after the first dance had ended, "will you take me now to the young stranger with the snake tattoo? Please, will you make my introduction?"

"How could I refuse the request of a daughter who has been so helpful in preparing for tonight's feast . . . and has prepared herself so handsomely?" asked Rabbit-Woman with a smile. Touching-Leaf's happy face burned bright as burnished copper. Putting an arm lightly around Touching-Leaf's waist, Rabbit-Woman led her to the other side of the bonfire.

After the two left, Sparrow-Song had little spirit to return to the dancing. Her legs and back ached already, after only one dance. She contented herself with watching the others as they told stories with their hands and feet, many times inventing the steps as they went along. After the men and boys had completed a dance pantomiming a deer hunt, Painted-Turtle came to her side.

"Why are you not dancing?" he asked with concern. "You allowed yourself to miss out on the Stomp Dance."

"No true reason," she stammered, uncertain what to

say. "Is this a new amulet?" she asked him, reaching out to touch a smooth stone in the shape of a turtle—Painted-Turtle's clan—pierced so that it could hang from his neck on a long cord of leather.

"Yes," he admitted, blushing. "I made it from onyx you found for me one day. In this way, you travel with me."

Both their heads then turned toward loud giggles. They saw Touching-Leaf and Gray-Feather on the other side of the bonfire, deep in conversation, their faces close to one another.

"I will miss our times wandering the woods together," she told Painted-Turtle sadly. "You are lucky that after your Vision Journey in the spring, your life will not change so much. When my time of courtship begins, I can no longer walk freely without a chaperone, either in the woods or the village, because it would be unseemly to come in sight of a man or a boy when I am alone. It isn't fair!"

"I wish I could change the way of things for you," said Painted-Turtle softly. Sparrow-Song thought again of courtship and a future husband, and wished it could be Painted-Turtle.

As the dancers grew smaller in number, Sparrow-

Song grew weary. Now she could not find her mother or her father or either of her sisters in the band of celebrants around the bonfire. Perhaps, she thought, they too had tired and already gone home. Only Winter-Sky remained, deep in conversation with a few of the visitors from the stony country. So, sleepy and fuzzy-headed, Sparrow-Song returned to her family's wigwam and fell into a restless dream.

Sparrow-Song awoke deep in the belly of the night. Her own belly throbbed with deep, dull spasms of pain. She felt warmth and wetness between her legs. Placing a hand on her inner thigh, she found it slick. It was her woman's blood, come for the first time.

Sparrow-Song fumbled in the dark for the bundle of supplies she had prepared for her first visit to the Women's House. She grabbed them up, along with her bearskin cover, and hurriedly dressed. The wigwam's packed-earth floor chilled her bare feet, despite the efforts of a smoky night-fire smoldering in its center pit. Glowing embers guided her past dark forms, snoring loudly, to her mother's side.

"Don't worry, little daughter," Rabbit-Woman

whispered sleepily, "I will come to you in the morning, as soon as I have prepared breakfast for the others. I will bring you something good to eat, and we'll talk."

Sparrow-Song silently crept through the wigwam's door-flap. She touched the totem pouch hanging around her neck, wishing for courage and guidance from her guardian spirits tonight. The idea of being alone, in exile from her family and home, filled her with dread. What a difference there was, she thought, between the joyful solitude of walks in the woods and the loneliness of this unfair banishment.

Once outside, she shivered. She wished she'd not neglected to pull on her moccasins before fleeing the wigwam. It was, after all, the time of the broken moon, when trees cast off the last of their leaves—soon the snow and ice of winter would come. But her flow had started, and it was now too late to return to the wigwam for forgotten items. Attracted by the scent of blood, a village dog loped toward her. He soon recognized that she was not a stranger who wished to do harm and let her pass.

The Women's House sat on the far edge of the village, close to the river. It was built much like her family's wigwam, but larger, and was surrounded by a tall fence of slender sapling poles. The poles were placed very close together and bound with hemp ropes so that no one could see inside. Sparrow-Song reluctantly pushed the gate open and walked into a small grassy courtyard. Was it homesickness already, or did she smell a fire burning inside the darkened hut?

Inside the Women's House, she discovered a tiny night-fire was, indeed, sputtering in its pit. Its dim light revealed that three of the sleeping benches were already occupied. Sparrow-Song was relieved to find she wouldn't have to spend her first night in the Women's House alone after all. Her totem spirits had answered her plea!

Quietly she searched among the supply baskets until she found one containing clean, soft, absorbent plant materials. Sparrow-Song took off her deerskin skirt and drew a long, thin strip of leather from her carry-bag. She tied it around her waist. She then took out a broader band of leather, laid it out flat, and placed a thick layer of cattail fluff on it. Then she carefully threaded it between her legs, and fastened it to her waistband, much like a breechcloth might be tucked. She wrapped and refastened her skirt around her, and headed for an empty sleeping bench. Stumbling, Sparrow-Song sent a pile of woven rush mats scooting noisily across the floor. One of the sleeping mounds stirred and sat up.

"Look who's here!" croaked Half-Moon as she shook the lump under a neighboring bearskin awake. "Ha! I told her it wouldn't be long before her first trip to the Women's House!"

"Even our father could have guessed it from her actions lately," yawned Touching-Leaf as she arose from the warmth of her sleeping bench.

"I thought I left you both sleeping in our wigwam, just moments ago," exclaimed Sparrow-Song, happy and puzzled at once.

"I had to come here right after the feasting, just as the storytelling began," explained Half-Moon. "I didn't even have time to tell Winter-Sky good-bye." Her voice grew vexed. "He was so busy entertaining our visitors, I doubt he has noticed my disappearance yet."

"But when did *you* get here?" Sparrow-Song asked Touching-Leaf. "As the dancing began, I saw you laughing with Gray-Feather on the other side of the bonfire. I could see how you charmed him, even from a distance."

"Yes, but I had to come to the Women's House before the dancing was even half done. I cannot believe my bad luck!" exclaimed Touching-Leaf. "Not to mention my embarrassment." She placed her chin sadly in her hands. "By the time I am out of my confinement, he will probably be gone, back to the stony country with his hunting party, and I will never see him again!"

"I am still puzzled," said Sparrow-Song. "If you are both here, who snores on the sleeping benches in our wigwam?"

"Guests, little goose," replied Touching-Leaf. "Two of the visitors to our village have taken our empty beds, of course." A sly smile crossed her face, visible even in the dim firelight. "I hope Gray-Feather sleeps on my bench!"

At that, all three sisters giggled loudly.

"Shh . . . ," cautioned Half-Moon, motioning over to the bed in the far corner. "Don't wake Meadow-Dawn. She needs her rest when she's here, with a sour husband and four squalling little ones at home." Touching-Leaf stretched and said, "We should sleep too."

But on the unfamiliar sleeping bench, slumber did not visit Sparrow-Song. Outside a distant wolf howled, calling her to join him under the stars. Wrapping her bearskin cover tightly around her shoulders, she drifted into the empty courtyard of the Women's House.

She built a fire in the outside pit and crouched nearby. As the flames sputtered and sparked to life, she looked into the face of the moon, yellow and waxy as summer squash. Someone long ago had strung small shells and hollow bird bones on strands of sinew and hung them in the courtyard tree. Rattling against bare branches in the brittle night wind, they sang a strange, soft song.

As she listened, she wondered what the path of a woman would be like for her. She would be expected to marry. She knew what would be expected of her on her wedding night, but she did not yet know what to expect of herself in this matter. Would her heart, and her body, move as one?

Sparrow-Song heard village dogs barking, and shortly thereafter, the gate to the Women's House burst open. Into the courtyard rushed the old medicine woman, Corn-Stalk. Leaning against her was a young woman clutching her swollen belly.

"Good, good," Corn-Stalk declared. "You've started the outdoor fire already. We will need plenty of warm water, to cleanse things and to prepare medicinal teas. Dancing-on-Water's time has come. Quickly, awaken the others."

This news startled and frightened Sparrow-Song. She had never attended a birthing before and was uncertain about what to do. Dancing-on-Water moaned. Although she was afraid of what was about to happen, Sparrow-Song saw even greater fear when she looked into the pregnant woman's wide eyes. Dancing-on-Water was only a few years older than she.

"Shall I help her inside?" she timidly asked Corn-Stalk. "Perhaps it would be good for her to rest by the night-fire."

"Yes, a good suggestion," agreed Corn-Stalk, who dashed ahead to shake the others from their slumber.

"Dancing-on-Water will need our help tonight," Corn-Stalk said with urgency. "She should have been here in the Women's House long before, preparing for her child's birth. But her own mother is ill with a fever and couldn't give her good advice. She came to my wigwam just now for help, when her pain is great. We must make things ready." Corn-Stalk turned to find Sparrow-Song cradling Dancing-on-Water's head in her arms, gently wiping sweat from her brow. "I see you have already found good work to do," she declared.

Corn-Stalk gave orders quickly to the others. Half-Moon would fetch water from the river, refilling the birch-bark buckets as many times as needed through the night. Meadow-Dawn would tend the fires, both outside and in, feeding them often so they would burn strong. Touching-Leaf was told to set a boiling pot on balancing stones in the fire outside, and to keep it filled, so they might have a steady supply of hot water for the work ahead.

Next Corn-Stalk rummaged through leather pouches containing her herbal medicines, the various dried and crumbled leaves, the many roots and stems crushed into powders. The old healer knew what each one was and how to mix them properly to achieve the desired effect. She measured a mysterious mix into the bottom of a wooden cup.

"When Touching-Leaf has boiled water," she told Sparrow-Song, "brew this until the tea is dark in color and cooled. Then give it to Dancing-on-Water to ease her pains. Encourage her to drink! I will return as quickly as these ancient bones will travel."

Sparrow-Song stiffened. "You're leaving?"

"I need more hands tonight, child, and I am the only one who may return to the village to get them," Corn-Stalk calmly explained. "With first babies, many hands are a wise precaution." She pulled a thick, short rope of rolled leather out of a basket and handed it to Sparrow-Song. "When her pains come, you must remind Dancing-on-Water to bite down on this."

"But . . ." Sparrow-Song looked fearfully into Corn-Stalk's weathered face. Fierce determination dwelt in its many valleys—kindness, too.

"You will not fail Dancing-on-Water, or her baby, tonight," Corn-Stalk said simply. "This, I know."

As the others busied themselves with their tasks, Sparrow-Song stayed by Dancing-on-Water's side. The pregnant girl began to writhe on the sleeping bench. "Would it ease your pain to walk awhile?" Sparrow-Song heard herself asking. Dancing-on-Water nodded yes.

Sparrow-Song held onto the pregnant woman and lifted her carefully to her feet, shouldering her ungainly weight so that she would not fall. She patiently walked the courtyard with Dancing-on-Water, pausing with her labor pains and asking often after her needs. The bones and shells, dangling from the tree and pushed by the wind, made music for their odd, stop-and-start dance.

Soon two older women of the village, who had borne babies of their own and assisted many others in childbirth, returned to the Women's House with Corn-Stalk.

"Why do you walk Dancing-on-Water? Who told you to do this thing?" Corn-Stalk demanded of Sparrow-Song.

"No one," she sputtered. "I'm not sure where the thought came from . . . but it seemed to help her. Have I done harm somehow?"

"Not at all," answered Corn-Stalk in amazement. "In my haste, I did not mention this comfort-giving practice to you. But you came to use it nonetheless. Your instincts are wise, child."

Together, Sparrow-Song and the women tended Dancing-on-Water. They gently massaged her back and legs. They placed medicinal teas to her lips. And when her last labor pains came, they urged Dancing-on-Water to grab tightly onto the birthing rope, to squat down at last and push. It was then that Corn-Stalk's strong, steady hands helped Dancing-on-Water's baby find its way into the world.

"Welcome, tiny girl," whispered Corn-Stalk as she cleanly cut the baby's cord. "All is well," she assured the new mother. "Rest now. The women will bathe your new daughter in the cold river waters, to ensure her body grows sturdy. I will bury her cord near the Women's House so that her heart will be bound, always, with her sisters of the tribe."

Sparrow-Song watched the sunrise with fresh wonder. Although the Women's House and its courtyard were not the wide, open spaces she loved to wander freely, she did feel a freedom here. She felt connected to life, too, in a strange new way. Maybe it was because of the help she'd given Dancing-on-Water during the dark hours of the night, or her witness of the dawning of new life.

Soon women from the village joined Sparrow-Song and the others. They admired Dancing-on-Water's infant daughter who, diapered in moss and wrapped in rabbit skins, dozed peacefully in a brand-new cradleboard. Some chanted blessings, others chatted by the fireside. All offered the new mother special treats forbidden to her in pregnancy, such as duck livers and gizzards, coaxing her to taste each. Being in the Women's House, thought Sparrow-Song, was not so much being cast out of the village as it was being in a village of another sort.

When Rabbit-Woman came with a morning meal for her three daughters, each one was eager to share her version of the night's events.

"Remember, you cannot eat anything with your fingers during your time in the Women's House," Rabbit-Woman reminded Sparrow-Song as she gave her two wooden sticks and the pair of moccasins she'd forgotten the night before. Suddenly ravenous, Sparrow-Song sprang upon the bundles nearly as fast as they were opened. Clumsily, her fingers struggled to keep each morsel balanced while bringing it to her mouth.

"You'll get used to the eating-sticks soon," Touching-Leaf promised.

"Not being permitted to cook food while in the Women's House is a good rule too," declared Half-Moon. "It pleases me not to wait upon a husband or to worry about pleasing him. It's good, for a few days, to do as I please."

"But doesn't Winter-Sky do things to please you sometimes?" asked Sparrow-Song.

"Judging from the sounds at night, under the bearskin covers, I'd guess so!" laughed Touching-Leaf. It was Half-Moon's turn to blush at a sister's remark.

"And may she be blessed with three daughters to give her white hairs," added Rabbit-Woman, "just like those on this old head!"

Corn-Stalk approached from behind and placed a veined hand on Sparrow-Song's shoulder. "This one shows good promise as a healer," she told Rabbit-Woman, in praise of her youngest daughter's help with the birthing.

Corn-Stalk gave Sparrow-Song a rare smile, one that revealed a softer side to the solemn, stern face she usually showed the world. "I thank the Great Spirit for sending you here last night, child. I have wondered often in the last few years, as I grow old, who might take my place as medicine woman for our village. Your actions have given an answer."

Sparrow-Song looked up in gratitude and surprise. "But I know nothing of poultices and plants!"

"A healer's skill first settles not in the hands or the head, but in the heart," replied Corn-Stalk.

"My spirit is willing, then, to learn all that I can," Sparrow-Song promised.

"Good, it is done," said Corn-Stalk. "We begin our lessons tomorrow, here in the Women's House." The old healer paused. "And, it would please me to serve as sponsor for your naming ceremony, when we welcome you as a woman of the tribe. I suggest the name Offers-Kindness. It suits you." Rabbit-Woman proudly nodded her approval.

"It's time to check on the needs of our guests," announced Rabbit-Woman, then, as she packed up the remnants of their breakfast. "Gray-Feather asks about you, Touching-Leaf. And Painted-Turtle stopped by for you, Sparrow-Song. Something about a *contest*?" Sparrow-Song quickly looked down and, with furrowed brow, pushed bare feet into her forgotten moccasins.

After Rabbit-Woman had bustled through the courtyard gate, Sparrow-Song sighed. "I'd promised Painted-Turtle a rematch, skipping stones at the riverbank today," she said to her sisters. "Now that I must be chaperoned, and our mother disapproves of this kind of unwomanly conduct, it will never happen."

Half-Moon and Touching-Leaf looked slyly at each other and then at their smallest sister. "I am a married woman, and therefore able to serve as chaperone for someone in courtship. Although, being new at the task, I may not look on as closely as our mother might!"

Sparrow-Song sighed again, but now with relief. She was no longer fearful about the woman's road that she was about to travel, for she knew she would not walk it alone.

the czarevna of muscovy
by Joan Elizabeth Goodman

long ago in the far-off land of Muscovy, the bells of St. Basil's Cathedral rang out for the Feast of Michaelmas. The tolling bells resounded in the vast Red Square, calling the Russian people to worship. The bells' insistent pealing penetrated the thick walls of the Kremlin, perched on its hill within the city of Moscow. The ancestral home of the rulers of Muscovy, the Kremlin housed palaces, parks, and churches for the imperial family and their attending court. Guard towers and church spires wore whimsical onion-shaped domes, gilt or sheathed in dazzling colored enamels. It looked charming from afar, but the Kremlin wasn't a pleasure garden; it was a fortress. For centuries its stout red walls had kept out invaders.

In her apartment in the Terem, the imperial palace of the royal family of Muscovy, Katya heard the cathedral's bells, and her heart beat faster.

"Please hurry," she urged her attendants. The bells called to her. The adventure of leaving the Terem was rare. She was eager to go in the carriage to the great cathedral, across Red Square, and see what little she might see of the world beyond the Kremlin's walls.

"Please, Czarevna, do not fidget," cajoled Princess Marta, who was pinning strands of pearls and emeralds into the plaits of Katya's raven hair.

Katya was the luckiest girl in the world. Everyone said so. For wasn't she the beloved Czarevna, the only child of the Czar, ruler of all Russia, and the beautiful and kind Czarina? No gown was too costly for the Czarevna. She dressed in plush velvet and silk brocade trimmed with sable and ermine. No delicacy was unattainable. She dined on larks' tongues, pheasant, caviar, kumquats, and crystallized ginger served on plates of onyx and gold. All the noble ladies of the Terem petted and spoiled her.

"How lovely is our princess this day," said Countess Ludmilla.

"She will make Their Imperial Highnesses proud," said Countess Yelena.

"The bells are ringing," said Katya. "I mustn't be late."

"The Czarevna will not be late," said Princess Marta.

And Princess Marta will not *be hurried*, thought Katya.

"How bright are your eyes today, Little Bird," said Baba Irina, the ancient healer, the *znakharka*.

"Today, will I see my heart's desire?" Katya asked the Old One.

"That I cannot say, Czarevna," said Baba Irina. "Keep your heart open and look about you."

"Where are the Czarevna's scented gloves? Where is her veil? Nina!" Countess Olga spoke sharply to the serving girl.

Nina ran to obey. Such was her life. All day long the noble ladies ordered her about. At night she lay at the Czarevna's feet and the two whispered secrets. When Nina brought forth the kidskin gloves and silken veil, the Czarevna was deemed ready. She was whisked down the grand staircases and into the courtyard where the imperial coaches waited.

The coachmen drew heavy curtains over the windows, lest commoners see the Imperial Princess. Katya peeked out through a small crack as her coach left the Kremlin and entered the Red Square. Rows of the Imperial Guard lined the coach's path to the cathedral. Behind them,

Katya caught glimpses of the Russian people bowing reverently at her passing. They were still and somber, and held little interest for the Czarevna. In the cathedral she would be able to study the beautiful icons while the priests droned. Perhaps some of the young nobles might be close enough for her to examine.

"What are you thinking, Czarevna?" asked Princess Marta.

"I'm hoping that there will be sugared violets at dinner." Katya kept her true thoughts to herself.

"Whatever the Czarevna desires," said Princess Marta.

In bed that night Nina whispered, "Highness?"

"Hmm?" Katya was nearly asleep.

"Did you find your heart's desire?"

"Oh, no," said Katya. "There was only Count Vladimir's spindly little boy."

"Too bad," said Nina.

"It will come in time," said Katya, as certain of it as day following night.

One day Katya would marry the noblest prince in Muscovy. With him she would rule over all the Russian people. A great future awaited her, but now her life was filled to the brim with samovar afternoons in the Terem; prayerful Feast days; lessons in letters, music, and etiquette; trilling with Countess Olga's songbirds; and being the delight of her parents. Although she asked Baba Irina to reveal her heart's desire, Katya was in no great hurry to find it.

The future seemed comfortably far off, but on the first full moon of winter following Michaelmas, in Katya's thirteenth year, the future came rushing at her. That next morning Princess Marta shrieked as she helped Katya out of her night shift.

"Run to the Czarina and bring her here," Princess Marta commanded Nina. "Tell her it is a joyful day, that of the Czarevna's first bleeding!" And she slapped Nina hard to impress upon her the importance of the message.

The blood shocked Katya, as did the excitement it caused. Was this bleeding what the noble ladies had been hinting at as they spoke increasingly of her impending womanhood? Katya's privates were washed and wrapped in muslin bands. And she was dressed in a new shift and robe. She felt most strange; her head throbbed, and there was a twinge low in her belly.

The Czarina came quickly, trailing a flock of noble ladies, and kissed her daughter.

"Can it be true, my little one?"

Katya curtsied for want of an answer.

Princess Marta threw back the coverlet to reveal the rust-colored stains on the sheets. She held up Katya's nightdress for all to see.

"Felicitations!" said Countess Ludmilla.

"A cause for celebration!" said Countess Yelena.

"Our little Czarevna has become a woman," said Princess Marta, and some delicate tears were shed.

Baba Irina arrived to examine Katya's stained undergarments. The ladies crowded around her, awaiting some pronouncement. Katya stood off to the side. She'd been fussed over her entire life. This was no different, and yet . . . she hated it. She couldn't respond to the well-meaning countesses. She even shrank from her mother's embrace. Couldn't they stop? But no, there was so little novelty in the Terem that they would seize on Katya's bleeding and worry it incessantly. This belonged to her, not them. Katya wanted time to herself to consider it.

She sighed, and Princess Marta was instantly attentive.

"You have pains, poor dear. Baba Irina will brew you a posset. Come, Old One, and help the Czarevna."

Baba Irina took her hand and studied her face.

"Make them go away," Katya silently pleaded. Baba Irina nodded.

"This child needs to lie down in peace." She spoke firmly. "And I will soothe her pains."

Katya felt no pain, only the oppressive solicitude of the ladies. Baba Irina shooed the ladies away. All except Nina departed. Baba Irina was about to send her away too.

"Let Nina remain," said Katya. The girl was quiet and discreet. "She will keep the others at bay."

"Well," said Baba Irina. "Are you in pain?"

"Not pain exactly."

"What would you have me do for you?"

"I know not. Only I feel smothered. I want to go out!"

"It is mild enough for a walk in the garden," said Baba Irina.

"Not the closed garden," said Katya. "Out, beyond the walls."

"You know that the noble ladies remain in the Terem Palace within the Kremlin except to go to St. Basil's Cathedral."

"I know," said Katya, "but my heart longs for something, I know not what, beyond the Terem, beyond the Kremlin's walls."

"It cannot be," said Baba Irina.

Katya threw herself on the bed and pouted while Baba Irina busied herself at the brazier. Nina sat quietly beside her in the corner.

"The ladies weren't always kept within the Terem," said the *znakharka*. "Before the Tartars' influence, the ladies of Muscovy lived as freely in the world as the lords."

"I wish I had been born long ago," said Katya.

Baba Irina put a towel steeped in rosemary across Katya's stomach.

"You must learn how to set your spirit free even as you remain in the Kremlin. For you have no choice but to live the life you are given."

The scent of rosemary calmed her. Baba Irina sang a lullaby of olden days in her crow's voice, and Katya was strangely comforted.

The bleeding stopped the next day. Katya's life resumed its customary course. She wore her elegant dresses, ate her dainty food, continued her lessons, and sat with the noble ladies, embroidering fine linen with silken thread. Yet as much as her life remained the same, that much it had changed.

The future Katya had ignored seemed suddenly thrust upon her.

"Now that you are a woman," said Princess Marta, "you must prepare more seriously for the duties you will share with the future Czar."

"Now that you are a woman," said Countess Ludmilla, "you must think of your duty to the Russian people."

"Now that you are a woman," said Countess Olga, "you must be good."

"And patient," said Countess Yelena.

"In time will come the blessing of children, and you will teach them as you have been taught," Countess Katerina assured her with smiles and loving pats.

Katya bit her lip to stifle screams of frustration. The more she heard of her future, the more she despaired. What good was Baba Irina's advice when her entire being would belong to others?

Yes, she would dine on larks' tongues, wear exquisite gowns, and perhaps her husband would be kind, but she would never live beyond the confines of the Terem

Palace. She would never see the world except through the Terem's windows. And her obligations to husband, to family, to the Russian people would constrict her more surely than walls of stone. Her desire to leave the Kremlin had grown into an unbearable longing.

"Walls and duties bind me," Katya lamented to Baba Irina. "The Kremlin is my prison."

"Fate binds us all," said the Old One.

Cold comfort.

Katya climbed the highest tower of the Terem. She looked east over the endless Russian plain to fields and villages dwarfed by the dark forests of Muscovy. Snow lay thick on the ground. Sleigh bells jangled on the troikas leaving the Kremlin. Drovers sang dirgelike airs as their heavy carts labored over the snow. Katya shivered as she watched faraway wisps of smoke from peasants' hearths curl and stretch up to heaven.

"There lies a world beyond the Kremlin's walls. Am I never to know it?" asked Katya.

The ladies of the Terem laughed.

"Why does she sigh for the world outside?"

"It is dirty."

"It is dangerous."

"It is only fit for tradesmen and peasants."

"The world of the Czarevna is within the walls of the Kremlin," said the Czarina.

Whenever she could escape from her increasing duties, her lessons, and the glowing tales of a future she loathed to think about, Katya trailed after Nina. Only with the servant girl was Katya spared the burden of her future.

Never before had Katya paid the servants any more heed than she did the chair she sat upon or the floor she trod. Now, following Nina, disguised in a muslin smock, Katya visited this world apart, yet within the Kremlin. Built into the massive walls of the palaces, the walls encircling the Kremlin, and tunneling under the streets was a warren of passages and stairways where all day and half the night servants scuttled, hidden from the eyes of those they served.

One day Nina led Katya to the underground laundry where a legion of washerwomen toiled so that the fine ladies and gentlemen had fresh linen every day. Bent over scrub boards, stirring steaming kettles, or ironing tiny pleats, the women sang. Katya listened, rapt, to songs of the great forests, the endless steppes, the whole vast land she would one day rule and never experience.

Another day Nina took Katya through the labyrinth to the kitchen gardens. In sheltered sunny corners and glass-covered sheds, gardeners coaxed plants to grow beyond their season.

"Have you anything to brighten the Czarevna's chamber?" Katya asked one of the earth-brown, silent men. He eyed her calmly, not seeing through her disguise.

He lumbered off and returned with a pale, pink rose.

"For the Czarevna," he said, bowing. "Give her this, the last rose of summer."

And it seemed to Katya the noblest gift she'd ever received.

The new moon's sliver waxed fuller nightly. The next full moon would confirm Katya's womanhood and her betrothal.

"Take me to the kitchens," said Katya after an interminable lesson on forms of address for foreign dignitaries.

"And what does the Czarevna desire?" asked Nina.

"What do *you* want?" asked Katya.

"Oh, Highness, I don't want . . . I . . ." Nina hesitated.

"Anything!" said Katya.

"Crystallized ginger!" said Nina, blushing.

"Then so it shall be!" said Katya.

They wove through the maze of passages to the cavernous kitchens, where cooks presided over vats of seething stews or roasting spits laden with venison and fowl, hissing and throwing off fat in the giant hearths. Bakers toiled in a hall lined with ovens. On long central tables they kneaded dough, crimped pastries, and built fabulous creations of marzipan and spun sugar. Hot-tempered cooks shouted orders and cuffed underlings who flew to obey.

"Pudding for the Czarevna with crystallized ginger," commanded Nina, her cheeks flaming. "And send the samovar at once! Her Imperial Highness wishes tea!"

They raced, stifling laughter, back to the Czarevna's apartment, arriving seconds ahead of the footman with the steaming samovar. As soon as Katya dismissed him, they fell into each other's arms, crowing with laughter.

"Send for the samovar!" shouted Katya.

"Post haste!" cried Nina.

Katya had never known such glee. The court ladies

were often merry. They twittered and chirped like Countess Olga's songbirds, but they never laughed out loud. It would have been considered crude.

Awakened to laughter, Katya's sorrow deepened, as each new discovery with Nina reminded her of the walls and the future that bound her. The lowliest peasant was freer to come and go than the Czarevna of Muscovy. Her betrothal loomed. A prince would soon be chosen, and she would belong to him. Katya couldn't recognize herself in the "woman" the court ladies kept insisting she'd become. She was happiest with Nina. Perhaps her true fate was to be a peasant.

Katya took Nina's small hand. "Promise me you will not tell of our escapades."

Nina sank to her knees. "Highness, I would rather die. I would die if anyone knew of this. I would be thrown into the deepest dungeon where the rats would eat me alive for leading the Czarevna astray."

"My friend," said Katya. "I would never betray you."

At the next full moon, Katya was wrapped in muslin bands and put to bed with a hot compress, although she felt perfectly well. The next morning Princess Marta was disappointed to find not even a drop of blood. The

Czarina and other court ladies were sent for. Baba Irina was summoned.

"What is the matter?" the Czarina queried Baba Irina.

"Nothing, my Empress," said the Old One. "The Czarevna is perfectly normal. Several moons may pass before the bleeding begins again. Or, it may start between the moons."

"Can you not brew her a potion, *znakharka*?" asked Countess Ludmilla.

"It is best to let nature take its course," said Baba Irina. "There's no sense in hurrying."

"Fear not, my dove," said the Czarina to Katya. "We will trust in the *znakharka*. I'm sure all will be well."

Katya felt she'd been given a reprieve. She sought out Nina as soon as she could escape the watchful eye of Princess Marta.

"Take me to a quiet corridor," she said. "I want to be away from all this fuss."

Nina led Katya through the maze of passageways to one rarely used. It was quite dark, cold, cobwebbed, and dusty, and as different from the imperial apartments as possible.

"Since the day of my first bleeding, all I hear about is

my glorious future," said Katya. "Yet this dark corridor may be the most exotic place I am ever to visit."

"Listen, Highness," said Nina. "There is more here than dust and spiderwebs."

Katya kept still and listened. A song, faint but clear, accompanied by rhythmic clapping came from the far side of the wall.

"Who sings?" she asked.

"See for yourself, gracious Highness." Nina unlatched a shutter Katya hadn't noticed in the darkness. She tugged with all her might, but the shutter wouldn't budge.

"Let me help," said Katya, impatient to see what lay beyond.

"No, Highness," said Nina. "You'll dirty yourself."

While Nina fought with the shutter, Katya's heart began to race. Beyond this window she sensed the answer to her disquiet. Would she find her destiny here?

At last Nina pulled the shutter free. Through the barred window came cold sunlight and an onslaught of sensations. Katya blinked against the vibrant colors. Wood smoke and cinnamon and the babble of a thousand voices rushed at her. In the enormous square brightly colored tents, wooden kiosks, and peasants' carts formed alleyways. Bonfires marked intersections. Despite winter's chill, the square, stretching all the way to the portals of St. Basil's Cathedral, was a surging, jostling crowd of people: Peasants bundled in bright red-and-blue wool like Matryoshka dolls, Eastern traders in turbans and quilted silks, and Muscovites swathed in furs were buying and selling a riot of goods, everything from exotic spices and jewels to poultry and pitchforks.

"Can it be the Red Square?" Katya asked.

"Yes," said Nina. "It is indeed the Beautiful Square."

Katya had never seen the Russian people so full of life, nor the square so lively and so unlike the solemn feast days. Nothing could have prepared her for this brilliant, raucous scene.

Right below her were the singers. Peasant girls, wearing fur-trimmed caps and embroidered aprons over layers of skirts, circled a bonfire. They skipped, stamped, and clapped as they sang. Their frozen breath wreathed them in clouds. Their feet marked out the time in fancy patterns on the ground. It was the most enchanting thing she'd ever seen.

"What are they doing?" asked Katya.

"They are dancing, Highness."

"That is what I want!" cried Katya. "That is what I must do!"

"But Czarevna, the priests say dancing is sinful. You know it is forbidden in the Kremlin."

"*They* care not what the priests say." Katya gestured toward the dancers in the square.

"They are only ignorant peasant girls," said Nina.

"I am behind bars, and they are free."

"Highness, these bars protect you from endless labor, hunger, cold, and soldiers who come in the night and—" Nina lowered her eyes. "I say too much. Forgive me."

"Only if you teach me this dance."

"Czarevna, I couldn't!"

"But you know how?"

Nina turned scarlet.

"You have to teach me."

"It would be terribly wicked, and so dangerous." Nina started to weep. "I'm sorry I brought you here."

"And I give my word, as Czarevna of Muscovy, that no harm will come to you, and no one shall ever know. Furthermore, I command you."

Nina sighed. There was no more arguing.

Katya learned quickly. Her feet already seemed to know the steps. Nina sang and they danced in the corridor. Katya would have stayed at the window overlooking Red Square until nightfall, keeping time with the peasant girls, but for Nina.

"Highness, you must return to your chambers. Princess Marta will call out the guard if you aren't ready for her to dress you for supper."

Katya let Nina lead her away, but even as they hurried along the dark passageways, her feet followed the pattern of the peasants' dance, and their song filled her ears.

The next day her bleeding came again.

"You see, my dove," said the Czarina. "All is well."

Katya nodded, not feeling well at all. She was swaddled and put to bed. This time she suffered true pains. Baba Irina and her brazier were brought to Katya's chamber. Princess Marta led the other ladies to the shrine of the Blessed Mother to pray and rejoice as the betrothal could now proceed. When Katya was alone with the *znakharka* and Nina, she clasped the Old One's hand.

"I have found my heart's desire!"

"And what is that, Czarevna?"

"I will dance in Red Square!" said Katya.

Nina blanched.

"No, Little Bird. That is not to be. You must put such a thing out of your mind now and forever."

"That I cannot do," said Katya.

Baba Irina sighed and spoke to Nina. "Take care, or the Czar will have you drawn and quartered."

Nina swooned.

"She has nothing to do with it," said Katya.

"Then you must protect her by letting go of this foolishness. You know that the priests would blame the girl and demand her death."

Katya turned her face to the wall and wept in frustration. Baba Irina revived Nina and prepared a drought for Katya's pains. Katya dutifully drank from the goblet Nina served her with shaking hands. The potion eased her into slumber.

Katya dreamt that the entire wall beside her bed was covered with a living tapestry in jeweled hues. It was like a great window onto Red Square, alive with a multitude of Russian people, just as she'd seen them in the bustle of market day. In the center of the square danced the peasant girls. At the same time, she could see through the Kremlin's walls the Czar and his court, the laundry women at their tubs, the gardeners with their plants, and the cooks in their kitchens. It was a happy dream, but Katya awoke in tears. She wept throughout the day and into the night.

Princess Marta and the other noble ladies were more attentive than ever. The Czarina left off her affairs of state to comfort her daughter. Nothing availed.

At midnight Katya fell into a troubled sleep. In dreams she saw Nina on a great precipice about to fall. She heard Baba Irina saying, "You've imperiled her. Only you can save her."

The next day Katya told Princess Marta that since she was a woman, it was unseemly to share her bed with Nina. "I want to reward the girl for her faithful service and send her back to her family."

The Czarina was consulted and agreed that the Czarevna might have the privacy she desired.

"I shall miss you, Highness," said Nina.

"And I you. But I have put you in harm's way. Return to your village and be safe."

Katya's eyes were dry, but her heart ached. She gave

Nina a purse of gold and an emerald brooch that would guarantee the girl's future.

They kissed, and Nina departed.

Once the bleeding stopped, Katya began to haunt the servants' passageways on her own. Day after day she sought the window that opened onto Red Square and could not find it. Despair was her constant companion.

As days passed into weeks, her feet forgot the patterns of the dance. Her heart forgot the song.

She barely tasted the delicate morsels on the crystal plates. In spite of Princess Marta's careful supervision of her wardrobe, Katya looked bedraggled in her velvet gowns. She could no longer attend to her lessons. She could think of nothing but the dance she had lost and the freedom she would never know.

"What could ail the Czarevna?" asked Countess Olga.

"What can be done?" Princess Marta worried.

Baba Irina brewed many potions to no avail. The third moon of winter waxed full, yet Katya's bleeding did not come. The Czarina prayed to the Holy Image of the Little Mother to help her troubled child.

Katya continued roaming the endless corridors without finding again the window to Red Square. If only

Nina could have safely stayed. She missed their secrets and their laughter. She missed her guide to the other world. Each time she passed Countess Olga's golden songbirds, she mourned their lack of freedom. One day she opened the cage and set them free.

"For shame!" said the Czarina.

"But, Mother, they have wings. They are meant to fly freely and not be shut up in gilded cages."

"They will freeze, or the hawks will hunt them. They will die out in the world," said the Czarina. "They are meant to sing their songs."

"In cages?"

"Yes."

"As we are meant to be shut up in the Terem?"

"Yes."

Another moon waxed to fullness and waned. Katya grew thin. Her black hair lost its luster, although Princess Marta dressed it with scented oils and brushed it until her arms ached. The bleeding did not come. The betrothal was postponed as rumors of the Czarevna's illness winged over the Russian steppes.

At the fifth moon, when spring seemed possible, the Czarina called for the court physician, who poked and prodded Katya, and prescribed black and bitter medicine.

Katya grew worse. The *znakharka* stayed by her side, soothing Katya as best she could.

"I shall die," Katya whispered in Baba Irina's ear, "if I can never dance in the sunlight."

The Czarina consulted the *znakharka*. "The court physician is useless," she said. "Old One, what will help my child?"

Baba Irina bowed deeply.

"Katya longs for what cannot be," she said.

"The Czarevna of Muscovy can have anything she desires," said the Czarina.

"She wishes to live beyond the Terem, outside the walls of the Kremlin," said Baba Irina. She did not tell the pious mother of the dancing, lest the Czarina think that demons possessed her child and lose all hope.

"The Czarevna cannot live outside the walls," said the Czarina. "But my child fades before my eyes. There must be something that will help her."

"If a cure exists, I will find it in the forests of Muscovy," said Baba Irina.

"Do whatever is necessary," said the Czarina.

While Baba Irina searched the forests, Katya

worsened. Her eyes grew dull, and her hands became so thin and frail the candlelight shone through them. The Czarina sat by her side, weeping tears enough to flood the Volga.

At last Baba Irina returned, her satchel filled with twisted roots, pungent bark, and wild mushrooms of Muscovy.

"Have you found a cure for Katya?" asked the Czarina.

"The cure depends on Katya," said the Old One.

She sent the Czarina away and prepared her brew by Katya's bedside. As the potion bubbled on the brazier, strange and wondrous odors wove through the Terem.

"Strawberries!" exclaimed Princess Marta.

"It is the scent of spring," said Countess Ludmilla.

"It is the smell of my childhood," said Countess Yelena, and she began to weep.

Katya's cheeks grew warm. She sat up without help and drank Baba Irina's potion. She felt herself growing lighter and lighter. By the time she'd drained the cup she was floating like a cloud above her bed.

"It is a marvel," said Katya. "I feel so well."

"Now you may seek your heart's desire and discover your true destiny," said Baba Irina.

"But I am already cured," said Katya.

"Not yet . . . not yet . . . not yet . . ."

Baba Irina's voice melted as Katya drifted down stairs and along the servants' passageways. She wove through the labyrinth, now certain of her path, to the dark corridor and the little barred window, overlooking Red Square. She was so light and thin she sailed easily through the bars and out to the marketplace.

She floated over the flower stalls, the Turkish rug dealers, the spice merchants from Samarkand, and the tea growers of Ceylon.

In the center of the Square danced a circle of peasant girls. Drawing closer, Katya saw Nina dancing with the girls. Her feet touched the ground, and Katya ran to join them. Their circle parted, inviting her in. Taking her place opposite Nina, Katya's heart filled with happiness. She began haltingly, but little by little her feet found the pattern. As she danced her arms and legs grew stronger. Blood coursed through her veins, and life returned to her.

Soon she flew around the circle with the rest. Around and around she went, her skirt billowing out like the onion domes of St. Basil's Cathedral. Her feet knew the pattern, and her heart remembered the song.

Nina smiled. "I knew you would come," she said.

Katya threw back her head and laughed. The other girls joined her, and the laughter became the refrain of their song. They danced until the sun went down.

One by one the peasant girls dropped in exhaustion until only Katya and Nina remained. Nina embraced Katya, picked up her pack, and began to fade into the dusk.

"Wait!" called Katya.

"I must go to where I belong, Highness. They are waiting for me."

"But the dance?" called Katya as Nina departed.

"The dance never ends," said Nina from far off.

Katya waved farewell to Nina's shadow and continued high-stepping and skipping. Her feet repeated the circle of steps as the mauve of twilight veiled the marketplace.

The merchants packed up their goods. The street sweepers whisked the cobblestones. The peasant girls shouldered their packs and headed for their villages. Only when the Square was empty and deep in the cloak of night did Katya notice that she was completely alone. And still her feet danced, her hands clapped, and her heart sang the tune.

When the bells of St. Basil's tolled the hour of midnight, Katya stopped dancing. All was stillness in Red Square. Everyone had gone to the place where each belonged. A few lights sparkled from the massive walls of the Kremlin, for generations the stronghold of the rulers of Russia. In the Terem, her mother would be leading her ladies in the midnight prayers of Matins. She'd be asking the Virgin Mary's guidance and help that she and the Czar might rule wisely and well. Katya's mother and father were responsible for each body and soul on the vast Russian plain.

Katya thought of all those who worked in the Kremlin who'd been hidden from her until Nina revealed them. She saw them all as she had in her dream. All those souls, the people who filled Red Square and the vast Russian plain beyond, would need her help and protection. Someday they would be her responsibility, just as the court ladies had promised. In becoming a woman and accepting that responsibility, she would gain, not lose herself. A worthy and noble life awaited her in the Kremlin. That was where Katya belonged. Now she understood that she could not and would not exchange it for the fields of the peasants or the caravans of the traders, even for the freedom to dance in Red Square.

Katya drew a deep breath, a breath of peace that filled the hungry yearnings of her heart. She had had her dance in the marketplace. Katya looked down at her feet. By the faint starlight she could see they were mere shadows. Her legs, her arms, her hands were all transparent. She was no more substantial than the night mist.

Baba Irina had given her a beautiful dream that she could keep forever. But she must go back. She could not abandon her destiny.

She returned to the Kremlin and her mother's waiting arms.

In time, Katya joyfully wed the most noble prince of Muscovy, and her husband succeeded her father as Czar. Katya was blessed with a daughter of her own. Although she was not free to roam the world, Katya had the world come to the Kremlin. Peasants, merchants, traders— people from all corners of Muscovy brought her their stories. Katya listened carefully and learned the heart's desires of her people. As the Czar's most trusted counselor, she worked to ease her people's burdens, to bring them security and happiness. She and the Czar ruled wisely and well.

Katya never again danced in the marketplace. But the dream Baba Irina had given her lived on, bringing her lightness and joy. Sometimes, when no one was around to see, her feet traced out a pattern on the marble floor. And when her own daughter was old enough to keep a secret, Katya taught her the dances of the peasant girls in Red Square.

Katya's daughter taught her daughter the steps. And so it went for generations, until there came a time when the Czarevna of Muscovy could dance openly in the Kremlin, and travel the length and breadth of her beautiful country and beyond, as freely as the birds.

sleeping beauty

by Lisa Rowe Fraustino

the day begins with a little kick of cramps in the belly. You ignore them and go to your eight o'clock biology class, a course designed to weed out the weaker pre-med students. You'd only miss it for your own funeral. The cramps can kick all they want; you won't let yourself feel them. The monthly peeling away of the uterine lining simply doesn't exist. You have more important things to think about.

You are on the straight path to your future, no time for getting off track. You are going to get a 4.0 this semester, graduate with the highest distinction in three more years, then go on to medical school. There you'll meet the man you will marry at age twenty-eight. Your medical school loans will be paid off and your first house bought by the age of thirty. By the time you're forty you'll have your own practice, or be a partner in one, and your two kids will be in school. After forty your future looks fuzzy, but you have plenty of time to plan that later. Vacations in Europe, investments for retirement, a second home, funeral plots so the kids won't have to worry about the arrangements.

After bio class you go to your job at the library. Returning books to the stacks, you feel a cramp. No, you don't. Your period doesn't exist. You need to work to pay the expenses left over after the scholarships and parental contributions. Besides, it would be ludicrous to ask your parents for the money to buy their Christmas gifts. The less debt you incur now, the more options you will have later. Maybe you'll be able to attend medical school at Harvard. That is your secret dream.

You go to lunch. The cramps kick for attention. You ignore them. You're not really hungry; you hate how fat you're getting; you'd rather get straight to work on the English paper you have due next week; but you know you have to eat to keep your blood sugar and electrolytes level. If you don't, you'll crash in the afternoon and have a difficult time paying attention to your history professor, who gives brilliant lectures at breakneck speed while your roommate's boyfriend sleeps in the back row. You know you should be used to it by now, but it takes you aback every time you see him or someone else fall asleep in class. You thought college would be different from high school, filled with serious students who really wanted to be there. Why is it that there are still more people who are dead to the world than there are people like yourself? Sometimes you feel all alone, even though inside you know you're not.

So you eat. Craving red meat, you settle again for a burger and fries despite the fact that you may suffer later for the grease. You never know how the cafeteria food is going to settle. It's a common problem, especially for freshmen. Your roommate's boyfriend calls every meal a crap shoot, ha ha. He's crass but correct. It's a mystery how you all manage to put on the freshman fifteen, considering how fast the food goes through. Maybe it's not the cafeteria where you put on your pounds, though. It's probably the parties.

You think you must have put on your extra fifteen pounds from one party alone, back in September, before you learned how to pace yourself. They had punch bowls of margaritas with gummy worms swimming on the bottom. You don't know for sure, since you don't remember a thing about that party after downing the first worm, but you figure you must have drunk most of a bottle of tequila by yourself. The hangover wore off in a couple of days, but months later you're still wearing sweatpants instead of your favorite jeans. You'll never make that mistake again. Now you rarely go to parties, and when you do you only pretend to drink. You stay in control of yourself at all times while you watch the rest of your fellow students unravel and unbuckle.

After lunch you stake out your favorite love seat in the library to work on your paper for English. It's your final paper, worth thirty percent of your grade, and you need to ace it since you got a B plus on the last one. You hate writing papers; the grading is so subjective, especially with assignments like this one:

Analyze your current life in relation to your favorite childhood fairy tale. Did your early preoccupations somehow predict the path you are on now? For instance, if you begged to be read "Little Red Riding Hood" over and over, do you now find yourself easily seduced by strange men? Or did the fairy tale teach you an important life lesson? When a hot boy tries to hook up with you at a fraternity party, do you recognize him as the Big Bad Wolf and give him the axe?

It's so annoying when frumpy professors in tilted

glasses and gray braids try to sound cool. Nobody over forty should say "hook up."

You have no idea what to write. At first you can't remember any fairy tales at all. You just remember the Disney movies, which your professor said you can only use if you also look at the original tales. Cinderella and her ugly stepsisters? No. Snow White and her jealous stepmother? No. They don't do anything for you. Beauty and her beastly boyfriend? Maybe. The girl in the Disney movie liked books. You like books. Was she a princess? You can't remember. You hope not. The fact that the beast turned out to be a prince doesn't bode well, but then again, Beauty fell in love with the guy for his personality, not for his looks. Maybe you can work with that. For about a week during junior year in high school, you thought you were in love with the school's biggest geek, complete with big nose, big ears, big zits, highwater black pants belted tight to his ribs. Beastly. But you were smitten with his brain, his wit, his talent. He has yet to wake up handsome, but by the time you graduated, he had turned his allowance into a tidy fortune on the stock market. A modern-day prince. He never gave you a rose, though. In fact, he never even noticed you. He only had eyes for Lara Kroft, Tomb Raider.

Nah, there's no paper in that. Not an A paper, anyway. You need to think of something good enough to maintain your GPA. What a stupid assignment.

You feel another kick of cramps. You go to the bathroom with a quarter for a pad, just in case, so you don't have to think about it anymore. It doesn't exist. So, when did you hear your first fairy tales? You close your eyes and drift back in your memory until you can feel yourself on someone's lap. Your mother's? No, it's your great-grandmother's. In a rocking chair. Your great-grandmother used to read to you out of a big thick book by the Brothers Grimm, pages yellowing at the edges. You breathed through your mouth to block out her acrid old-lady smell, but you loved hearing her grainy voice, feeling her soft warm body surrounding your little wiry one, watching her trembling thick-knuckled hands turn the pages, veins blue under the liver spots. Did you even pay attention to the tales themselves? Did you have a favorite?

Bunches of kids used to gather around when your great-grandmother read at family gatherings. Now the voices come flooding into memory. One cousin begged to hear "Hansel and Gretel" over and over. The cousin liked the part where Gretel pushed the witch into the oven. You were horrified at your cousin's delight. It was as if you were baking your own mother. No, what you liked was imagining Briar Rose asleep in the tower while all the kings' sons came and tried to get through the thorny hedge into the castle. You giggled at their futile efforts to win a pretty princess they had never met. Served them right! Then one day the thorns turned into a hedge of beautiful flowers that parted of their own accord to let Prince Charming pass. You made a yucky face when he kissed her and she woke up. It reminded you of your dog. Your dog used to wake everyone up in the morning with sloppy kisses.

So that's it. "Sleeping Beauty." How embarrassing—a princess story was your favorite after all. Why on earth did you, of all people, identify with a beautiful princess passively awaiting her prince? You take such effort— pride, even—in controlling your fate. Is there something passive lurking within you that you can't see? The story has gotten under your skin now. You must look deeper to find the forgotten child who sleeps within you.

What else do you remember about the story? The curse, of course. The evil fairy cursed the princess to fall down dead when she pricked her finger on a spindle at age fifteen. Aha! Sleeping Beauty got her period! No wonder they call it the curse. Of course, the last good fairy was able to change the curse of death to a deep sleep of a hundred years. The other good fairies had already given the princess their gifts, gifts that made her just about perfect—beauty, wit, grace, talent in dancing, singing, and playing music.

The blood rushes hot to your face. Oh God. That's you, sort of. You're often told you're beautiful. You feel fat now, what with your extra freshman fifteen, but you do have a pretty face. And you're talented. Not that you're a natural at everything—you have to work at it—but you have all the gifts the fairies gave the princess. Valedictorian, Sandy in *Grease*, drum major for the marching band, humor columnist for *The Bee*, and even Clara in *The Nutcracker*, back in the days before some activity had to go. But all that perfection didn't happen by magic, a gift from the fairies. You *have* to. Be perfect. There's a hunger inside you driving you to achieve, and you work like a fiend to feed it. Failure is not an option.

Success is not its own reward but a stepping stone to a higher goal.

Did you like "Sleeping Beauty" best because you were a budding perfectionist? An overachiever? It wasn't even about the prince at all, not for you—because you didn't even understand that part. You were too little to know what the wake-up kiss stood for: S-E-X. But you understood the importance of the gifts the fairies bestowed: S-U-C-C-E-S-S.

You've got your A idea: "Briar Rose, the Gifted Princess." Excitement carries you to the computer to find the original tale on the World Wide Web. The teacher loves it when you quote details. A *plus*. You are not having cramps. Your uterus does not exist. On the Web you find a site with all sorts of Sleeping Beauties, different versions of the tale. Voraciously you read. It doesn't take long before you are taken aback, though, like hearing your roommate's boyfriend actually snore in class.

There are details that don't belong in the story, awful details that should not be told to children. They certainly weren't there in your great-grandmother's tellings. Maybe some ignoramus typed it wrong for the Web page.

You go to the stacks and dig the actual books out to make sure you're reading the authentic brothers Grimm version, the version your great-grandmother used, the loose-paged book itself still treasured by one of your aunts. Yes indeed, you're looking at Grimm's. But how could this be? Your great-grandmother never told you the princes who tried to rescue Sleeping Beauty got caught in the thorns and died a miserable death. You were never told that in some versions of the tale, Sleeping Beauty is woken by more than a kiss. You were never told that Sleeping Beauty sometimes awakes several months after the prince's visit to find herself suckling a child.

This is horrifying. Your mind floods with an unwelcome image of yourself waking up naked on a cold, spinning floor beside a strange boy. You shake the image loose and sign off the computer with a deep uneasy feeling. It's time to outline the history chapter for this afternoon's class.

At section II. B. 3., the first jackknives slice through your stomach. Damned hamburger. You ignore the pain long enough to finish the outline, but each page brings more knives. Instead of going to the history class, you go to your room and curl up in bed. Sleep is the only cure for the cafeteria bellyache, you know from experience. Sleeping and waiting for the end. You sleep between the waves of pain, paring knives, then steak knives, then butcher knives. You almost welcome the cleaver, because that will signal the frantic run to the bathroom that will purge you. Cafeteria food gives new meaning to "the runs," says your roommate's boyfriend.

Except this is not like the other times. The cleaver does not purge the system as usual but instead comes back again and again, in waves too close together for sleep. At one point the pressure becomes so great that your bladder releases in a helpless gush that feels like gallons. Such loss of control has never happened to you before. How humiliating. You hope the fluid doesn't seep down through the mattress onto your roommate's bunk, where you know she does it with her boyfriend when you're not there. You are saving yourself for marriage, or at least for engagement. Your life plan allows no time for the emotional entanglements that result from physical entanglements.

At some point you lose your lunch. You didn't expect that. Cafeteria food doesn't usually go both ways. Maybe it's not the grease after all. Maybe you just have the flu.

Your roommate gets home and fusses over you. Her boyfriend told her you weren't in history class. Everyone who knows you likes to tease you about how Ms. Perfect never misses class. Even the Monday after that wormy margarita party you don't remember, you went to class. There must be something terribly wrong for you to be in bed instead of in history class, your roommate says. She's caring and teasing at the same time. If laughing didn't hurt right now you'd tease her right back. Once every month she has something terribly wrong. Her boyfriend calls it the manufacturing of vampire tea bags. She stays in bed the day the cramps hit, moaning and crying softly. It's not as if she's going to bleed to death. She hasn't learned to ignore herself yet.

As if she knows what you're thinking, your roommate says hopefully, "You might be getting your period." That's irrelevant. Even if you were, that wouldn't phase you. You're just sick, you tell her. You're okay. But you let her go for Pepto-Bismol. It sometimes stops the knives. You're in the bathroom when she gets back with the medicine. It doesn't help. This is wearing you out. All you want to do is sleep.

No use returning to the wet bed now. Not worth the effort. Might as well just stay slumped on the floor by the porcelain throne until the end. Nothing but pain has passed through you for the past several waves, but you still feel like you have to go. Have you ever been this tired in your life? Maybe the day you were born. You're glad you don't remember that.

Sounds echo off the mirrored walls. Teeth are brushed. Showers are taken. Toilets are flushed. A blanket is pushed under the door of your stall. Girl after girl asks what's wrong. Do you want to go to the infirmary? The emergency room? Finally you give up telling them you're just sick and scream for everyone to leave you the fuck alone. They understand. Many a party girl has spent the night wrapped around her porcelain lover.

You are left alone.

Music from the surrounding dorm rooms vibrates in the ceramic tile, its rhythms getting into your bones. You feel it as a throb of numbness. You are being drowned out. The pains are no longer felt. You feel as if you are outside your body, looking down on yourself curled limply in fetal position, your eyes closed between the waves that tighten your body in knots, your mouth open during the screams.

And finally, as the darkness wraps the dorm tight in the quiet night, you feel it, with a knowing as sure as the cycle of moons—the pain is nearing its end. Somehow you gather the strength to pull yourself up into a squatting position, back against the stall door, bare toes gripping the grouted tile. Your muscles push against the pain, push it out of your body, purge you of its weight. The final explosion of pain feels almost like pleasure, the greatest pleasure of your life, far better than what you imagine a prince would give, but the release takes your last bit of strength. You don't even have the energy to look, to see what came out of you. But you don't need to look. You know now. You could have known all along if you wanted to. You still don't want to know, but now you have no choice. There it is, gasping for its first breath.

You lie back down. Your lifeblood drains slowly, quietly, onto the hard white floor, and at last you sleep.

transfusion
by Joyce McDonald

mona stares at the abandoned bag of groceries on the kitchen table. She digs through the bag looking for the coffee and pulls out a warm carton of milk instead. She can't believe Danny brought the groceries this far, then left the milk to sour. At the moment he is in the living room with his study buddy, Becca Chapman. Danny actually calls her this. Mona calls her Danny's "study bunny," which pisses him off.

Desperate for a caffeine fix before she leaves for work, Mona pulls the rest of the groceries from the bag and sets them on the table. No coffee. She checks the refrigerator. The coffee can is still there. She shakes it to confirm it's empty, then slams it into the trash can under the sink.

Becca's airy laugh drifts in from the other room. Mona's instinct is to cover her ears. She knows this is silly. The two of them are, after all, just studying for a chem exam. Instead she occupies herself with stacking cans of extra hot chili—Danny's latest food fetish—in the cabinet next to the stove.

On nights like tonight, when she has to work the eight to two shift at the psych hospital, Mona knows Becca is going to hang at their apartment. To *study*.

Each time Mona crosses the room to put away more groceries, she averts her gaze from the open doorway leading to the living room. But something about the way Danny's voice goes suddenly soft draws her attention to the two forms sitting on the couch by the front windows. Danny is at one end, Becca at the other. Her body, curved comfortably into the corner, is turned toward him. Her long legs are stretched out in front of her. Her shoes are on the floor. She is wearing striped socks so bright that Mona can see the colors from across the room. Yellow. Orange. Red.

When Mona came through the door a few minutes earlier, Becca didn't even look up from her book. The flit of her hand was more a dismissive wave than a greeting. Mona knew she'd caught them off guard, coming home from the library instead of going straight to work as she'd planned. But she forgot her lit book and has a test the next day. She tried to explain this, but Danny cut her short, saying he was sorry he hadn't put the groceries away yet.

Mona stands in the doorway, holding a carton of eggs. She wants to tell Becca to get her stupid, smelly feet off their couch—the couch Mona and Danny discovered by the road in front of someone's house—but she doesn't dare. Becca and Danny would think she was nuts. Why give Becca ammunition?

Mona still remembers the day she and Danny found the couch. Together they carried, shoved, and dragged it seven blocks, taking breaks along the way, sitting on it, much as Becca and Danny are now. They pushed and pulled it, panting and grunting with each step, up the three flights of stairs to the empty living room of their apartment above an old landmark theater, and made it their own. Christened it that very afternoon with sweat from their skin. Mona can still remember the feel of Danny's hands coming between her and the scratchy upholstery, sliding along her naked back, lifting her body to his.

They have been living together since the end of their freshman year. Danny is the first man—the only man—

Mona has had sex with. She wants to trust him. She wants their relationship to work. But one morning, the week before, when Mona came home from working the graveyard shift, she thought she smelled Becca's scent—almond soap and sex—on her pillow when she climbed into bed. Without a second thought, she stripped off the pillowcase, took it into the kitchen, and set fire to it in the sink.

By the time Danny woke up, Mona had disposed of the ashes and scrubbed the sink raw with Comet. Danny stood in the doorway, sniffing the air. "Is something burning?" he asked.

"Toast," Mona said, before she remembered the toaster was broken.

She wonders now why she didn't wave the pillowcase right under Danny's nose and demand an explanation, wonders why she burned the evidence—if that's what it was. Except for the queasy feeling in her stomach every time she sees Becca and Danny together, she doesn't have much else to go on.

Becca looks up from the book in her lap and smiles over at Danny. Neither of them seems to be aware of Mona lurking in the kitchen doorway. Becca stretches one leg and rubs her bright sock-covered toes along Danny's thigh. Danny glances up at her from his chem book and smiles. He rests his hand on Becca's foot and gently strokes it.

Every muscle in Mona's body howls for immediate retaliation. Only . . . she can't seem to move. And suddenly there is Danny, crossing the room, coming toward her. Like Becca, he isn't wearing shoes. In fact, he is barefoot. *Theoretically* Mona understands the strategic importance of the surprise attack. Danny's family, Irish to the core, knows how to get in the ring and knock out their opponents before they see it coming. He has shouted her into head-spinning silence on more than one occasion. Mona feels the smooth Styrofoam egg carton in her hands. The weight of it. *Theoretically* she understands she is holding a potential weapon. She closes her eyes.

She can see the action unfolding so clearly.

Carton open. Eggs launched one at a time. Eggs flying fast and furious. Two hit the door frame. One sails past Danny's head. He stands in the doorway in jeans and a T-shirt, arms folded in that way that makes his biceps bulge. She lets loose another egg. This one hits the top of the doorjamb. The smashed shell and its contents slide down the wood and land on Danny's head. Yolk and egg white spread across his gelled hair and dribble down his forehead. She laughs.

When Mona opens her eyes, the carton of eggs is still in her hands. Lid closed. Eggs intact. Danny stands barely two feet away, frowning at her. Behind him, from the couch, Becca watches both of them with interest. A tiny smirk stretches the corner of her mouth. The carton of eggs slips from Mona's grasp, landing by Danny's bare feet. Yolk and eggshells splatter in all directions.

He jumps backward. "What the hell's the matter with you?" he says, swatting sticky eggshells from one foot then the other.

Mona stares down at the mess on the floor. "You forgot the coffee," she says, because it's all she can think to say at this moment. She points to what's left of the groceries on the table. "We're totally out. How am I supposed to function tomorrow morning? I've got the eight to two shift tonight." Traitorous tears sneak into the corners of her eyes.

Danny looks dutifully chastised. He steps around the yellow goo in his bare feet, coming toward her. His arms are outstretched. Mona's body tips slightly in his direction. She could fall into those arms without a second thought. Lose herself completely, as she always does when his body touches hers. But as he reaches for her, Mona pulls away. If he says one word about Becca or her striped sock on his thigh . . . if he tries to explain . . . with Becca right there in the other room . . . but Mona doesn't give him that chance. She grabs her backpack from where it sits on a kitchen chair and heads for the door. It feels good to race down three flights of stairs.

"Hey!" Danny shouts. He hangs over the railing. His face is a white blur surrounded by spiky dark hair much like her own, only shorter. She hears the muffled thumping of his bare feet on the steps behind her. He follows her out to the sidewalk. The lights on the marquee are winking at them.

Mona doesn't slow down.

Danny runs alongside her, trying to keep up. "This is about Becca, isn't it?" He puffs the words between breaths.

When Mona doesn't answer, he says, "This is all some bullshit idea you've got in your head." He taps his temple with his finger. Rapid gunfire taps.

Mona doesn't trust herself to talk right now. She can

barely think straight. And Danny's already on the offensive. She's not ready for a confrontation. She picks up the pace.

Danny's footsteps slow. He has stopped following her. Mona feels his absence. The air where his body had been traveling alongside her has become colder. If she looks back, which she doesn't dare do, she knows she will see him standing there, looking lost and confused as he tries to decide what to do next. In the end, she knows he will go back to the apartment. He will wash the dried egg yolk from his bare feet. Maybe pour himself and Becca glasses of the diet Pepsi Becca always brings with her. Maybe put away the rest of the groceries, although Mona doubts this. And then he will give his study bunny his undivided attention while she tutors him in covalent bonding.

Mona hates chemistry. She dropped the class after two weeks.

The campus bus pulls away just as Mona reaches the corner. It will be at least fifteen minutes before the next one comes along. Mona's anxious feet won't let her stand still for that long. She has to keep moving.

It will take her a half hour to walk to the other side of

the campus, across the river where the medical school and university hospital are. She doesn't have to be at work until eight and it's only seven fifteen. She keeps walking. She cuts through the quad, picking up her pace as she jogs down the hill past the biology building to the bridge that spans the river. Mona doesn't stop until she reaches the center of the bridge. She looks out over the river, a muddy tear that slices through the center of town.

It is already dark. The air from what began as an unusually warm October day now nips at her hands and face. She is wearing jeans and only a light sweater over a T-shirt. But there is no way she's going back to her apartment for a jacket. The wind picks up, tugging stubborn yellow leaves from branches and sending them downriver.

Mona pulls a lint-flecked tissue from the pocket of her jeans and blows her nose. Her throat is thick with tears, clogged with words she was too afraid to say to Danny. If she confronts him, and her suspicions about Becca turn out to be true, then what? Mona doesn't want to think that far ahead. It's like thinking about her own death.

She stuffs the soggy tissue back into her pocket and

rests her hands on the cold railing. It has been a dry summer and fall. The river has been low, the motion of the water slow, almost lazy. Mona isn't fooled. She knows what it can do. Last March, when she was still a freshman, Mona watched the river grow violent with the spring thaw. Saw it toss ice blocks the size of pickups onto the banks, heave them against tree trunks.

Tonight the river seems anxious, seems to be picking up speed. She has heard reports of heavy rains farther north.

As the full moon sends eddies of shimmering light bobbing along the rushing water, Mona is reminded how, on such a night, over a hundred years ago, when the university wasn't more than a handful of stone and brick buildings, when forests and rolling fields of wheat and corn circled the campus and the streets of the town were rock-hard dirt, a girl named Liddy Dolan, on the eve of her sixteenth birthday, weighted down with three heavy coats, each belonging to her brothers, plunged from the bridge where Mona now stands.

Like everyone on campus, she has heard how, on the night Liddy died, the river turned red and bled fish for three nights and four days. The fish lay in the hot sun on the riverbank, rotting, their eye sockets hollow. Their dried flesh crunched beneath footsteps like dead leaves. The rancid smell settled over the town and the university, and the air vibrated with the loud buzzing of millions and millions of flies. They nested in the dead fish. They blackened the riverbank.

Mona breathes deeply, half expecting to smell the rotting fish. She cocks her head and listens hard. She has heard how, ever since that tragic night, women crossing the bridge—women in pain—sometimes hear the buzzing sound in their heads. Feel it beneath their skin.

She wonders if Liddy's story is true, wonders if her lover betrayed her, as some believe. Did he leave her for someone else? Did the river offer her a refuge from her pain?

Mona rubs her upper arms and stares into the tumbling water below. What will she do if her instincts are right? What if Danny really is having sex with Becca? It's not as if Mona can kick him out. The apartment lease is in both their names. And it's not as if she has somewhere else she can go, or someone else she can stay with. She hasn't spent much time making friends since she came to the university, just a few casual acquaintances from her classes.

Something dark is tossing about in the water. For one heart-stopping second Mona thinks she sees a body tumbling along with the current. But it is only a log. One thick branch reaches upward like the arm of a drowning person.

She watches the log bump against a concrete pile beneath the bridge. First one end, then the other. It doesn't seem to be able to get beyond this point. She waits a few minutes to see what will happen, but it's getting late and the log doesn't seem to be making any headway.

It isn't until she sits down at the front desk across from the sliding glass window that looks out into the reception area that Mona realizes the only book in her backpack is her French text. Her lit book is still back at the apartment. Ordinarily she would have called Danny and asked him to bring it to her. She looks over at the phone. If she calls, he might think she is trying to pry him away from Becca. Mona can't get the image of Becca's striped-socked foot sliding along Danny's thigh out of her head.

Her legs begin to twitch. They bounce on the balls of her feet. Her fingers are scarcely an inch from the phone. She crushes them into a fist.

She is about to jump up and do laps around the four desks in the office when the phone rings. "Behavioral Health Center," Mona says, trying to sound cheerful.

A voice yells back, "I can't get that yolk shit off the linoleum. It's like Crazy Glue or something."

She swings the desk chair around so her back is to the sliding glass window. "Deal with it," she says.

She can hear Danny sucking all the air out of the kitchen. "Better yet, hand Becca a sponge and a bottle of Fantastik. At least she'll be doing something—" Mona is about to say, "Something more than screwing my boyfriend while she's there." Instead she clamps her hand over the mouthpiece. The sound from the other end of the line is like air hissing slowly from a balloon.

"What's that supposed to mean? 'Doing something'?" There's an edge to Danny's voice. He's getting ready to light into her. Mona can tell.

"Nothing," she says. "Forget it."

"You think something's going on between Becca and me, don't you?" When Mona doesn't answer, Danny yells, "That's *nuts*! You're like delusional or something. Maybe you should talk to one of those shrinks you work with."

Mona isn't about to get into this with him on the phone. And some small part of her can't help but wonder if maybe Danny is right. Maybe it is all in her head.

"Becca went home," Danny says, backing off. His voice gets lower, softer. "We need to talk about this, Mona. Only not on the phone. Come home. Okay? Tell them you can't work tonight. We'll talk."

Danny isn't winning any points with this one. It doesn't matter to Mona that Becca has gone home. She always goes home eventually. And she always comes back. It suddenly occurs to Mona that maybe Danny wants the best of both worlds—her *and* Becca.

One of the patients begins to pound on the doors. The patients are sequestered in rooms somewhere behind double doors that lead from the reception area to a hallway and to yet another set of double doors. The pounding booms down the corridor into the reception area.

Danny is still talking, still pleading. But Mona holds the phone away from her ear. For some reason her heart has picked up the beat of those pounding fists. A few seconds later the pounding from the inpatients' ward stops. It has taken up residence in Mona's head. Danny's voice has begun to sound like a harsh echo in a tunnel. Mona hangs up the phone.

She feels the patient's angry fists behind her eyes—feels as if those fists have suddenly grabbed onto her ovaries and are squeezing the life out of them. She massages her lower abdomen to ease the cramping. The clock above the door reads 8:15. Five hours and forty-five minutes to go. She circles the office, pulling open desk drawers. Not one of the full-time day staff has so much as a bottle of aspirin in their desk.

Through a throbbing haze of pain, Mona notices someone standing at the window, a young woman with long black hair fanning out from the sides of her head. Wild wind-blown hair. Mona presses her palms against her eyes, fighting the sharp pangs.

The girl at the window hums softly to herself. She sways back and forth to her own music.

"Are you looking for someone?" Mona asks.

The girl gives her a faraway smile and closes her eyes. Mona wonders if she is on something. Ecstasy maybe.

The girl drifts over to a chair and stares down at it. She runs her hand along the back. "I'm not going back to him," the girl says. "He's a liar." She has stopped humming and has her head turned toward the sound of Mona's voice, although she doesn't look directly at her.

"Who?"

When the girl doesn't answer, Mona says, "Have you been here before? I mean, are you seeing one of the doctors?"

The girl nods. "Yeah. Dr. Mentes."

Mona knows Dr. Mentes only by name and reputation. He is the head of the psychiatric department. She has never met him in person.

The glare from the fluorescent lights in the office reflects off the glass window, making it difficult to see. Mona slides the window open a few inches. "Is he your doctor?"

The girl, who Mona guesses to be about her own age, shrugs and goes back to humming to the chair. Mona sees that she is wearing white shorts and a shimmering red sequined V-neck top that comes only to her belly button. Not exactly mid-October attire. She has on high platform sandals that cause her body to tilt forward. She looks as if she might tip over at any minute.

Mona's instinct is to help the girl into a chair before that happens. But she is not allowed to open the office door to anyone except the medical staff. "Do you want to talk to the doctor on call? I can page him."

When the girl doesn't answer, Mona decides to page the doctor anyway. She doesn't want to handle this by herself.

A few minutes later Jeremy Atwater comes through the doors. The second he spots the girl in the white shorts, his eyes roll back in his head. The look he gives Mona suggests that the presence of this person is somehow all her fault.

Mona rubs her temples and thinks about asking Dr. Atwater for some Tylenol but then decides this wouldn't be a good time.

Dr. Atwater takes a seat a few feet from where the girl stands with her hand curved around the back of the chair, as if it's resting on someone's shoulder for support.

"What's the problem tonight, Evie?"

Mona watches them from the window as Evie tilts an ear in Dr. Atwater's direction without looking at him.

She picks at the back of the chair. Her fingers work fast, moving back and forth, flicking invisible somethings into the air. Mona decides Dr. Atwater has probably treated Evie before. He seems to know her.

"Why don't you sit down," he says, pointing to the chair Evie is single-handedly attempting to pick apart. She takes a step back. From the look on the girl's face, Mona thinks she might bolt for the front door. But then she slumps into the chair. She rocks her legs back and forth, bumping them at the knees.

Dr. Atwater is trying hard not to look at those restless legs. He keeps his eyes focused on Evie's face. Even with a throbbing head and cramps, Mona finds this funny.

Evie is tugging at the sequins on her top. She manages to pull one loose, but it still hangs by a thread. She goes to work on another. Then another. Until Dr. Atwater says, "Evie, have you been taking your medication?"

Evie stares at the wall behind him.

"Evie," Dr. Atwater says, softly. "Did you understand my question?"

"*He* took them," Evie says. "He takes *everything*."

Mona leans on the counter on her side of the window. She doesn't even try to pretend she's doing something other than listening to their conversation. She wants to know who took what from Evie.

"Took your medication? Someone took it away from you?" Dr. Atwater asks.

The phone rings. Mona glares at the intruder. She doesn't want to miss what's happening in the reception room. Dr. Atwater turns his attention to Mona. His heavy dark-rimmed glasses flatten his features. He's waiting for her to silence the phone.

Mona sighs and picks up the receiver. Danny's voice bellows over the line. "What the hell was that for?"

"What?"

"Why'd you hang up on me?"

It occurs to Mona that it has taken Danny ten minutes to call her back. If it took him that long to get his courage up, it could mean he knows he's wrong and he's feeling guilty. This isn't a comforting thought.

"Listen," Dr. Atwater says to Evie, "I can't help you if you won't talk to me."

Mona watches Evie rise, cut a wide path around Dr. Atwater, and head over to the couch.

"Mona? Hey, are you still there?" Danny says. "Don't hang up again, okay?"

"Do you want to sign yourself in?" Dr. Atwater asks Evie. No answer. "Or . . . I can set up an appointment for you as an outpatient. Would that work?" No answer.

Mona presses her hand against her own throat and listens closely to Evie's silence. She feels her pulse beating beneath her fingers.

"I'm coming over there," Danny says.

Mona holds the phone away from her ear and stares at the receiver. She isn't ready to talk to Danny about Becca. Not yet. And not while her head is pounding.

"No," Mona tells him. "Don't. I'm working. There's a patient here. And one of the doctors. I have to go." She hangs up.

Her head is throbbing worse than ever. "You got any Tylenol in this place?" she calls over to Dr. Atwater. "My head's about to explode."

He glances down at Evie, who has gone back to plucking at the red sequins. "Yeah, I know what you mean."

"I'm serious," Mona tells him.

Dr. Atwater comes over to the window. He tilts his head in Evie's direction. "I can't do anything for her," he says. "Not unless she signs herself in. And I can't force her to do that."

"Who is she? What's wrong with her?"

"Her name is Evelyn Rojas. She's one of Dr. Mentes's patients. She has schizophrenia. Paranoid schizophrenia. She spent some time in here as an inpatient last year. She's in the outpatient program now." He looks over at Evie. "She's either off her meds or they need to be adjusted."

"Well you can't just leave her there," Mona says. She is feeling a little panicky.

"Evie, I think you should go home now. Don't you?" he tells her.

Evie doesn't hear him. She doesn't even look his way. She seems to be having a conversation with someone who isn't there. Or at least no one Mona can see.

Dr. Atwater shrugs. "Maybe you can get her to go home," he says, and heads for the double doors.

"Hey!" Mona shouts after him. "I'm not the professional around here."

But Dr. Atwater has already escaped through the doors. Mona knows she can forget about his bringing her any Tylenol. He's going to avoid the reception area for the rest of the night if he can.

Evie curls into a ball on the couch and closes her eyes.

Mona goes back to her desk and opens her French text. She can obsess about Danny and what she should do, or she can practice conjugating irregular verbs with a pounding headache and cramps. Either way, it's painful.

It is almost one in the morning when Mona hears the sound of fingernails rapping on the glass. When she looks up, Evie's pale face, framed in her wild black hair, stares back at her.

Mona's hand rests on a sheet of notebook paper. Beside it are five more pages, covered on both sides with her sprawling, loopy handwriting. She has spent most of the night writing a letter to Danny, telling him how she feels about him and Becca. Danny has called seven more times in the past four hours. Each time Mona has told him she can't talk to him now. Instead she has written this letter. Danny can't shout words off a page. He can't render a piece of paper speechless.

Evie shifts from fingernails to knuckles and the rapping grows louder. Mona goes to the window. Up close she can see that Evie's hair—the wildness of it—is actually a tangle of unwashed, uncombed strands.

"Call him," she tells Mona.

For one confusing moment Mona thinks Evie is talking about Danny. "Who?"

"Dr. Mentes," Evie says. The red sequins glitter under the fluorescent office lights. Mona imagines herself in a glittery top like Evie's. She has never owned something with sequins on it. She wonders if Becca has any sequined clothes. Wonders if Danny has ever seen her in them.

"It's after one in the morning," Mona tells her. "He's going to be pissed if I wake him."

"Wake him." Evie sounds so in control, Mona can't believe it's the same person.

"I don't have his home phone number." This is a lie of course, but Mona doesn't want to call anyone at this hour unless it's life or death.

"Page him, then," Evie orders.

It's at least fifteen minutes before Dr. Mentes answers the page. Mona tells him about Evie. When he says to let the intern on call handle it, she tells him what Dr. Atwater tried to do.

Evie is circling the reception area, gently patting the backs of all the chairs as if they are the downy heads of children.

"Does the phone reach over to the window?" Dr. Mentes says. Mona can tell by his voice that he's not happy about this call.

She lifts the cord and gauges the distance. "Yeah, I think so." The throbbing in her head has become almost unbearable.

"Let me talk to her, then."

Mona carries the phone over to the window, dragging the cord along. She sets it on the counter and gets Evie's attention, which is no easy feat. She hands the receiver to Evie, who cups her hand around the mouthpiece and turns her back to Mona. She can barely make out what Evie is saying, her voice is so low.

Just as Mona is about to return to her desk, Evie says, "He wants to talk to you." Her arm extends through the partially open window. The receiver dangles limply in her upturned palm.

"Make an appointment for her to see me tomorrow morning," the voice barks at Mona.

"What about now?"

"Now? It's one thirty in the morning. This isn't an emergency. I told her if she thought it was to sign herself in."

"No. I mean, what do *I* do now? Evie doesn't want to leave." In fact, Evie is leaning on the counter on the other side of the window, plucking strands of hair from her head one at a time, examining each one closely, tossing it aside, and then going for another. Mona flinches each time Evie yanks out another hair, but Evie doesn't so much as blink.

"You get off at two," Dr. Mentes says. "It won't be your problem after that."

Good point, Mona thinks. In a few minutes she will call a cab. She tells Dr. Mentes no problem, she'll make an appointment for Evie. Even though she doubts Evie will keep it. She suspects Dr. Mentes knows this too. She hangs up and heads over to the computer.

"What's a good time for you to come in tomorrow?" Mona asks Evie.

Evie gives her a blank stare. "He told me not to come here anymore."

Mona has brought up the screen she needs to schedule Evie's appointment. She is ready to type in the information. She isn't sure she heard Evie correctly. "What?"

"He said it screws up my head," Evie says.

"Who said that?"

Evie stares at Mona as if she expects her to know the answer to that question.

"Right." Mona has no idea what to do next.

"I'm not listening to you anymore!" Evie shouts over her shoulder to no one in particular. "You *lied* to me. You *tricked* me." Mona feels as if she's intruding on someone's private phone conversation. She types in Evie's name and gives her a nine A.M. appointment with Dr. Mentes. She writes the information on a little card and hands it to Evie through the window.

Evie stares at the card in Mona's hand, then pockets it in her shorts, no questions asked. She begins to pace around the reception area, arms flying in agitation. She is going on about how Dr. Mentes is really a demon. How it's the white coat that fools everyone. It has magical powers. When he puts it on, he looks like a normal human being. Without it, he's a monster.

Mona is on the phone with the cab company when she realizes Evie's monologue about the demonic Dr. Mentes is actually part of a conversation directed at her. Evie stands at the window, arms crossed on the counter, waiting for Mona's reaction.

Alex Griffin, who is working the two to eight shift, comes through the front door as Mona is hanging up the phone. He takes one look at Evie and says, "Oh shit." He has been working in this ward for over a year. Mona's guess is that he has had encounters with Evie before. She buzzes him in even though, like her, he has a key.

Alex leans over her as she bends down to get her backpack. Mona smells beer when he says, "How long has she been here?"

"Since sometime after eight." She fills him in on the details. Evie has gone back to pacing the reception area.

Alex stands there frowning and cracking his knuckles. Mona folds up her letter to Danny, stuffs it in her backpack, and slides the strap over one shoulder. "Good luck," she tells him. She has decided to wait outside for the cab. Never mind that it's cold and that she doesn't have a jacket. Evie is Alex's problem now.

She is almost through the front door when she hears Alex roar at Evie to get the hell out. And that's just what Evie does. She tears through that front door faster than a bullet through butter. Mona can't believe this is all it takes. She might have been grateful to have this piece of useful knowledge if Evie weren't suddenly beside her, clinging to her arm, and trembling all over.

"He didn't have his white coat on," Evie whispers. "I could see his demon face."

"Alex doesn't wear a white coat," Mona says, as if this were a normal conversation.

"I know. That's why I can see him. The *real* him."

Mona wonders if all this time Danny has been wearing a white coat, figuratively speaking, of course. What would she see if he took it off? She rubs her arms and thinks about the jacket she left back at the apartment. She is freezing in her light sweater. Evie must feel like a block of ice in her shorts and sequined top.

Mona wishes now that she had spent more time making friends on campus. If she had, maybe she'd have someplace else to go tonight, someone to talk to about Danny, someone to help her figure out what to do.

She looks over at Evie, who has turned away from her and is babbling incoherently to the air. For a brief moment, Mona finds herself actually envying Evie. At least Evie has her hallucinations to keep her company. People she can talk to, even if they aren't real.

Across the road, beyond a patch of grassy park, the

river shimmers beneath the full blue-white moon. The bridge, outlined by hundreds of lights that are reflected in the water, seems to Mona in that moment to be all that is holding the two opposite sides of the riverbank together. Without the bridge, Mona has the feeling everything will fly apart. She watches it, hoping to see the headlights of the cab.

Evie has stopped babbling and is watching the bridge too. "Some people think it was because of her brothers." Her warm breath rushes into Mona's ear.

"What?"

"Liddy Dolan. I mean, it's true her brothers tried to keep her from seeing that guy. But that isn't the reason she killed herself."

"What guy?" Mona still has her eyes on the bridge.

"She was in love with this student from the university," Evie says. "He was from Boston. The guy was a real prick."

Surprised by the sudden shift in Evie's voice, Mona turns to her. She wants to know more about "the prick."

"Why did she do it, then? Kill herself."

"Because of him. The *prick*. This one night she snuck out after her father and brothers were asleep. She walked over three miles to the campus just to be with this creep. He was waiting for her in the old carriage house. They climbed into one of the carriages. Liddy wanted him so bad, she told him she would do anything for him. *Anything*."

Evie weaves her fingers together and presses her locked hands against her chin. "They did it. You know? Had sex. Liddy thought they'd be together forever. She thought he'd take care of her. But it turns out the guy was seeing this other girl from some snotty finishing school in Boston. They were practically engaged. After that night in the carriage, he acted like Liddy didn't even exist."

"How do you know this?" Mona asks.

"I talk to her sometimes."

Mona looks longingly at the bridge. She is willing that cab to appear with all her might.

"He must have told some other guys what happened," Evie says, "because Liddy couldn't walk down the street anymore without some sleazebag wanting her to go down on him.

"So this one night she put on her brothers' coats, not for revenge like some people think, but because they were heavy and she'd sink to the bottom of the river faster." Evie hammers her clamped hands against her chin.

"Then she went up on the bridge and—you know—jumped. I guess she couldn't figure out any other way to stop the pain."

Mona stares at Evie. Why is she even listening to this? She knows Evie hears voices, is probably delusional, and no doubt hallucinates. Despite all that, Mona says, "It sounds like the guy was a real jerk."

"Yeah," Evie says and looks away.

Mona has a feeling that this isn't Liddy Dolan's story, except for the ending maybe. It's Evie's. Evie, who seems to be drowning too. From the inside out.

Something swells in Mona's chest, making it difficult to breathe. Fifteen minutes have passed since she called for the cab. She tries to focus her attention on her watch, but all she can think about is Danny gently stroking Becca's foot as it danced along his thigh.

Mona knows that when the cab finally does show up, she will have to go home. Home to Danny. Home to Becca's scent on her couch and maybe her pillowcase. It suddenly occurs to Mona that maybe she burned that other pillowcase more out of fear than anger. She wanted to make it all go away—Becca's scent, the evidence, the dread of a confrontation. Without the confrontation, things would go on as if nothing had changed. Now she sees that she has been deluding herself. She squeezes her eyes closed. But Evie digs her fingernails into Mona's arm, forcing her to open her eyes again.

Mona looks up to see headlights approaching. She is so relieved she wants to hug the cabby. Her tour of duty has ended. "You have an appointment with Dr. Mentes tomorrow at nine," she calls over her shoulder to Evie as she opens the cab door and climbs in.

Before she can close the door, Evie slips in next to her. She slams the door shut with surprising strength.

The cabby turns his red jowly face to them. "Where to?"

When Evie says nothing, Mona gives the driver a general address, an all-night hangout called the Burger Barn. She doesn't want Evie to know where she lives.

Mona thinks about calling Danny on her cell phone and asking him to meet her there. She doesn't want to walk home from the Burger Barn alone at two in the morning. She reaches around to unzip her backpack and get her phone. She knows if she calls Danny, he will think everything is okay between them. And she will have to pretend that, for now, it is. It's either that or walk those five blocks by herself. Mona's hand folds around the phone. It feels smooth and cold. She slides her fingers over it a few times but doesn't lift it from the backpack.

The driver steers the cab onto the bridge.

The lights along both sides seem to flicker on and off inside the cab as it begins its journey to the other side. Mona blinks at the alternating light and shadow. The temperature in the car seems to have plummeted. Evie stares out the window with her palm pressed against the glass. She mumbles something about the smell of dead fish. Mona sniffs the air. It smells more like dead cigarette butts, dirt, and male sweat.

"Hear that?" Evie whispers. She is suddenly alert—spine straight, eyes wide.

"Hear what?"

"That buzzing."

Mona wonders if Evie feels the same buzzing beneath her skin that other women claimed to have felt when they crossed the bridge. A prickling sensation dances up and down Mona's own arms and legs. The lights from the bridge are creating a strobe effect inside the car. She has the strangest feeling that the cab is crashing through time and space. If that were possible, would she see Liddy Dolan climbing up on the railing, ready to jump? Would she take her hand and plunge with her to the bottom of the river? Let the water swell her belly, her lungs, her throat until there is no room left for pain?

A soft wailing sound pulls Mona from her fantasy. Evie has her hands clamped over her ears and is rocking back and forth. Mona tries to calm her down, but Evie lunges toward the front seat just as the cab thumps onto the road on the other side of the bridge. "Tell me you don't hear that!" she shouts, grabbing the cabby's shoulder.

"Lady," he barks, "I'm trying to drive here. Sit *down*." The car swerves slightly as the cabby shoves Evie's hand away. "You better control your friend," he warns Mona. "Unless you want us to end up a pile of twisted organ donations."

Mona would like to tell the cabby that there's no way she can control this Evie person. She barely knows her. She would like nothing better than for him to stop the car right now and let her out. But she's still over a mile from the center of town, it's the middle of the night, and her cramps are getting worse.

She reaches for the waistband of Evie's pants to pull her back, but not before she sees a blotch of blood the size and shape of a very small banana on the seat of Evie's white shorts. The blood has begun a slow trickle down her left thigh. Mona has the bizarre feeling that she is watching Evie's life oozing from her body.

Evie, too, has become aware of the blood. She scrapes her hands up her thigh, trying to wipe it away. When Mona tries to make her sit down, Evie grabs her arm. Without looking, Mona knows there is now a bloody handprint on her sweater. Evie's hands travel over Mona's face, leaving bloody fingerprints on her cheeks, like the markings of a warrior intent on battle.

"He said he'd take care of me," Evie says, leaning close to Mona. Tears stain her cheeks. "But he doesn't. He makes me . . . he makes me . . ." Evie's voice trails off in a sob.

"Makes you what? Who does?"

Evie doesn't answer. She has begun to shake all over. "I'm not going back," she says.

Mona is shivering too. She thinks she understands

why Evie came to the psych hospital, why she followed her into the cab. Like her, Evie has nowhere else to go. "You shouldn't, then," Mona says. Her breath comes out in white clouds. Together their breaths have fogged the windows. Mona can't imagine how the cabby can see to drive.

She tries to put her arm around Evie's shoulders, to calm her, but Evie can't keep her hands still. Bloody fingerprints are everywhere. Mona reaches for the fluttering hands, but they slip from her grasp, leaving streaks of blood on her fingers. Evie clamps her hands over her ears again. There is blood in her hair. "Oh God. That buzzing." She begins to moan. Softly at first. Then increasingly louder. A horrible sound that reminds Mona of a cat in heat.

The sudden piercing squeal of brakes brings Evie's moans to a halt. "That's *it*," the cab driver yells. "Out! Both of you. *Now!*"

Fog has coated all the windows. Mona has no idea where they are. She opens the door on her left. Across the street is the Rite Aid Pharmacy. Her bearings come back to her in a rush. They are on Main Street, less than half a block from her apartment. Mona slides out of the cab and slams the door. She doesn't look back. The cab driver rolls down his window a few inches to take her money. He snaps the dollar bills from between Mona's bloodied fingers, almost closing the window on them.

Mona hears a thump and sees a red palm pressed against the window. Evie is still in the cab. The glare from the overhead streetlight blots out Evie's face. In the seconds before the cab peels away from the curb, spitting dirt and stones from beneath its tires, Mona sees only her own reflection, her own eyes, her face streaked with bloody fingerprints—her warrior face. The face Evie has given her, like some external blood transfusion, a face ready for battle.

She looks down the block toward the theater. The marquee lights are off, but the lights in her apartment are still on. Danny stands at the window, a dark faceless shape outlined by the dimly lit room. He is waiting up for her. Waiting to talk. It is time. And Mona is ready.

maroon

by Han Nolan

i was eight years old when I learned the facts of life from
my cousin, Candy Sue Valentine, and those facts changed
both of our lives forever. It was 1969, the same year the
twins were born and Mama got her first car, a maroon
Buick station wagon. It was also the year I learned what
maroon was. I loved the word and I went about the house
saying it every chance I got. My daddy made me leave the
dinner table once because I kept saying it—maroon,
maroon, maroon. I wanted Mama to paint my room
maroon, but she didn't have any time for painting things
after the twins were born. She didn't have time for much
of anything besides the twins.

Mama said Candy Sue was coming to help her take
care of the babies, but when I got a look at Candy Sue that
hot day in July when she first arrived at our home in
Alabama, I wondered how much help she was going to
be. She had long blond hair that she wore straight and

parted down the middle. She wore blue jeans, but they weren't overalls like mine and Daddy's and they weren't work jeans like my mama's either. These jeans were long and tattered bell-bottoms that dragged on the ground when she walked, and they were tight all the way up her skinny thighs. Her shirt was kind of like a sack, long and shapeless with fancy embroidery on the front. She was holding a stuffed teddy bear that I thought might be a gift for me, but it wasn't; it was for her own self. She was fifteen, all grown up in my eyes, and there she stood holding tight to a teddy bear, staring at me and pouting. Mama and Daddy didn't allow pouting in our house, but they didn't say anything to Candy Sue. That alone should have tipped me off that something unusual was going on, because it didn't matter if you were the queen of England: If my mama or daddy didn't approve of what you were doing, they let you know straight away.

Candy Sue and her family had moved up north to Philadelphia before I was born, so I had never met her before. My daddy had to drive two hours to the airport in Birmingham to pick her up. I wanted to go meet the plane and get me an ice-cream cone on the way to the airport, but I had to stay home with Mama and the twins, so the first time I saw Candy Sue was when she stepped out of the new maroon Buick.

I went up to her and said, "Howdy," and she just stared down at me with her squinty silver gray eyes and didn't say a thing. That left me feeling awkward, like I had done something wrong, but I pretended I didn't notice, and I said, "Candy Sue, let me take you to your room." I took her free hand and led her toward the house. "You've got to share a room with me," I said, leading her up the stairs to the bedrooms, "or else you've got to sleep with the twins, and they'll keep you up all night with their crying and carrying on, so even though I'm only eight, I think you'll be happier with me. Later on I can play the piano for you. Did Daddy tell you that I was really good on the piano? Mama has to drive me all the way to Homewood, which is almost to Birmingham, just to get me lessons."

"Well, whoop-dee-doo," Candy Sue said in a pouty-sounding voice. I learned later that "whoop-dee-doo" was one of her favorite expressions. It always made me feel stupid, so I tried to say things that wouldn't get that kind of response, but it was hard. At least she had sense enough not to say it to my folks, probably because she'd tried it with her own folks and got herself smacked for it. No, she just saved them all up for me, kind of like the way I saved up the word maroon for when I was alone and could listen to myself say it without getting into any trouble. I figured she just needed to hear herself say whoop-dee-doo a lot. I tried it out and it was kind of a fun word, but I, too, had enough sense not to say it around my mama and daddy.

When we got to my bedroom, Candy Sue looked down at the light blue shag carpet with all its magic marker stains and then at my Barbie dolls and Barbie's Dream House all set up between the twin beds, and she set her hands on her hips and sighed. I moved over to the Dream House and knelt down beside it and said, "You wanna play?"

Candy Sue didn't answer. She walked over to the beds and kicking the nearest one with her foot asked, "Is this one with the Cinderella bedspread mine?"

I nodded. Then she flopped down on the bed and stared up at the ceiling with her teddy bear still in her arms and said, "I have landed in the pit of Hell."

I was about to warn her that we didn't take the word Hell in vain. You had to be talking about God and Heaven and sin if you wanted to use that word, but my daddy showed up with Candy Sue's suitcases and I had to wait and tell her later. After Daddy left us I told her how we didn't use that word and we also didn't use the words "shut up" or call anyone a liar. If someone were lying to you, then you said they were telling a story. Candy Sue glared at me and said, "Shit," and I said, "Yeah, that's another word we don't say around here."

Two things I noticed about Candy Sue over the next few days were that she spent a lot of time in the bathroom, and she wasn't any good at helping Mama with the twins or anything else. Most of the time she sat on her bed with the table fan blowing straight on her face listening to the Rolling Stones sing "As Tears Go By," over and over on my Walt Disney suitcase record player, and writing letters to someone named Scott Freeman. She always put on a smear of shimmery pink lipstick when she finished each letter and sealed her envelope with a fat kiss.

One day Mama and Daddy and the twins went into town and left me at home to practice my piano, expecting Candy Sue to watch over me. She didn't watch me at all. I didn't know why, but anytime I played the piano she went off and hid herself away, like she thought my playing was just that awful. She claimed that the piano was too out of tune, and it was painful for her to listen to it. I said what would she know about it, anyway, and she answered, "Didn't your parents tell you anything about me before I came here?"

I said, "No, why?"

"It figures," she said, not answering me and taking off in a huff for the bedroom. And that's where she stayed anytime I practiced.

Since she wouldn't watch me that afternoon when my parents were gone, I watched her. She was in the bedroom sitting on the bed, listening to "As Tears Go By" and smoking a cigarette. I could smell the smoke all the way into the living room, but both my mama and daddy smoked, so I didn't think they'd notice anything different when they came home. Candy Sue had turned the music up so loud I couldn't practice, so I wandered into the bedroom and sat across from her on my bed and stared at her sitting with her teddy bear in one hand and her cigarette in the other, listening to her music with her eyes closed. A freshly sealed envelope lay beside her on the bed, ready for the mailbox. She had tucked her hair behind her ears, so I stared at the gold stud earrings she had stuck into the holes in her earlobes. I had always wanted pierced ears, but Mama said pierced ears looked tacky on a white person, so I couldn't have any, but I thought they looked awful pretty on Candy Sue, and her skin was white as cotton.

When the song was over, Candy Sue opened her eyes and leaned forward to start it over again. She caught me staring at her and tried to hide the fact that I had startled her just sitting there when she didn't even know I had come into the room.

"Well, what?" she said, sounding disgusted with my very presence.

"You're too young to be smoking."

"Are you the police?"

"It will stunt your growth."

She laughed and said, "Good! That's just what I want." Then she squinted at me, and holding her cigarette out to me said, "Want a drag?"

I leaned back. "No! If my daddy knew you offered me a puff on that he'd turn your hide to leather."

Candy Sue laughed again and said, "Big whoop-dee-doo."

I looked at her hugging that teddy bear of hers and wondered why she loved that bear so much, so I asked her and she said, "Why shouldn't I; don't you think he's cute?"

I shrugged. "I guess, but the twins are lots cuter and you don't even say boo to them. You act like they don't even exist, and you're supposed to be helping Mama. I help her more than you do."

"You hear your mama complaining?"

I grabbed my own stuffed bear and held it in my arms. "No. But then why don't Mama and Daddy send you back home? How come you're really here?"

Candy Sue blew out a puff of smoke. "I'm just biding my time until my boyfriend comes."

"Your boyfriend?" I pointed at the envelope by her leg. "You mean that Scott Freeman? If he's your boyfriend, how come he never writes you back? Every day you run out for the mail, but so far nothing's been for you."

"That's only 'cause our parents are trying to keep us apart. That's why they sent me to this backwoods hick town in the first place. But nothing's going to keep us from being together. Someday real soon he's going to come riding down that dusty dirt road you call a driveway and grab me up, and we're going to go get married." Candy Sue leaned forward and stubbed out her cigarette on one of my saucers from my tea party set.

I stood up. "Hey, that's real bone china there, you know," I said.

"Well, whoop-dee-doo," she said.

"Shut up!" I said, feeling my face getting hot.

Candy Sue looked at me and laughed, but it wasn't her usual snotty laugh. She laughed in a way that made me feel that she liked me, and all of a sudden I didn't mind that she was using my china tea set for an ashtray. I laughed, too, and said the forbidden word again. "Shut up, you—you big whoop-dee-doo!"

Candy Sue giggled and lit up another cigarette. She handed it to me, an offering of friendship. This time I took it and held it for a second between my two fingers the way I'd seen my mama do it, and I felt all grown up. I took a drag and choked on it, but then I took another smaller one and I didn't cough at all. I crossed my legs like a lady and started to take a third puff, but then Candy Sue's laughing expression changed and her face twisted up in anger and she swatted the cigarette from my hand.

I watched it fall onto the shag carpet and Candy Sue jumped up and stubbed it out with the ball of her bare foot.

"Hey, what did you do that for?" I asked, stunned.

Candy Sue looked up at me and she, too, looked stunned. Then her face relaxed, and she picked up the cigarette off of the carpet and sat back down on the bed. "Look," she said, setting the cigarette next to the other one stubbed out on my china plate. "Don't be in such a hurry to grow up, okay kiddo?"

I uncrossed my legs. "I'm not," I said.

Candy Sue sat pretzel style in the center of her bed. She swept her long hair behind her and looked me over, tears welling in her eyes.

"You don't know how lucky you are to still be just a little girl. In a few more years you'll get boobs and get fat, and then you'll get your period, and it's all over after that. Your whole life stops, only you don't know it. You think it's just the beginning. You're a woman, you think. You believe you're all grown up, but don't be fooled, okay? Just don't be fooled."

"Okay," I said. "But what's that? What's your period? Isn't that what you said?"

Candy Sue told me, but I didn't believe her. How could we bleed from down there and not die? I didn't want her to know how scared I was about what she was telling me, but I was horrified.

"You're just trying to scare me," I said. "But I'm not scared because I don't believe a word of what you're saying, and I'm telling Mama on you." I backed away from her, moving all the way back onto my bed until I was up against the wall hugging my teddy bear.

Candy Sue shrugged and put the record on again. "You'll see," she said.

I had heard "As Tears Go By" a million times by then, but that time was different. I listened, and I felt so sad I thought my heart would break, and yet I didn't know why. I cried and Candy Sue came over and climbed onto my bed and held me and cried too. We rocked and cried, and in the back of my mind I hoped she would tell me she was just kidding about the bleeding, but she didn't and I knew I believed her. I knew I had believed her from the start. I remembered once, long before the twins were born, I had gone to the bathroom right after my mama had gone, and even though she had flushed the toilet, there was something left behind in the bowl, something white and bloody with a funny string floating out from one end of it. I flushed it away and forgot about it until that moment rocking and crying with Candy Sue. Yes, I believed what she had told me, but I vowed to myself that it would never happen to me. I vowed I would pray every night to God and God would hear my prayer and it would never happen to me. I would never get my period. I would never ever bleed down there.

For several days after that afternoon I kept my distance from Candy Sue as much as I could. I didn't know why. I guess I thought if I spoke to her again she'd tell me more horrible things, and I was still trying to absorb what she had already told me. How could a woman bleed for five days straight and not die? Candy Sue said it was blood we didn't need in our bodies unless we were making a baby. She said the blood was for the baby. But if it was blood we didn't need, then how come it hurt so much? Candy Sue said that it was so painful some months that she would almost faint, and sometimes it made her vomit. She said she had a friend who bled for eight days every month! Did Mama bleed like that? Did Mrs. Brambley, our neighbor?

I studied my mama a lot that hot July, looking to see if

I could tell if she were bleeding and getting ready to faint, but everybody looked faint that summer. It was one of the hottest summers ever, and that's saying a lot in Alabama. I still can remember the slow quiet way we all moved through the minutes of each day. There was no place outside shady enough to get comfortable and away from the humidity that made us feel all wrung out and limp, so we spent most of the time indoors in bare-floored rooms with wicker furniture, and ceiling fans whirring and humming above our heads.

I practiced my piano every day with a floor fan blowing on my back and read Nancy Drew mysteries and helped my mama with the twins. They were cranky in the heat, and Mama and I would take them outside and hose them down beneath the big magnolia tree out back every few hours and then pat them dry and place them in their cribs to sleep again.

When my daddy came home each evening from his shoe and leather repair shop, I hung around him out in the garage and handed him tools and refills of iced tea while he worked on a beat-up Rolls-Royce he once won at a poker game he played down at Roy's barbershop.

All during that hot July I felt a strong need to stay

close to my folks, especially my mama, and out of the blue I would hug her and tuck my head down against her chest, and she would say things like, "Well, what in the world?" and "I declare, child, what's come over you?"

The truth is I was worried about her. I was afraid for her. I didn't want her to bleed to death. I would watch her sitting on the sofa in the late afternoons with both babies in her arms, shaking them up and down to keep them from crying, or feeding them, or sitting with them out on the porch swing, singing them a sleepy little song while they screamed in the heat, and she looked so worn out. Her forehead would be damp with sweat, and no matter how much hairspray she used, her hair would go limp and flat as the day wore on, as if it just didn't have the energy to sit on top of her head all the hot day long.

Candy Sue spent most of those days waiting by the mailbox, pacing back and forth with an umbrella in her hands to keep the sun off her head. No letter from Scott ever came, so every afternoon she'd march back up to the house, throw the mail down on the hall table, and run off to my bedroom to cry and listen to "As Tears Go By."

Mama and Daddy tried to get Candy Sue to participate in the family and help out with the chores instead of sulking by the mailbox every day. Mama showed her how to hold both the babies at once in a way that kept their heads supported, which she said was very important so their necks didn't snap and break; and she taught her how to get the formula just the right temperature, and how to diaper them and bathe them without pricking them with the safety pins or drowning them in too much bathwater. Mama even taught Candy Sue how to cook her famous fried chicken, which we ate cold with a Jell-O mold with peas and pineapples floating around inside. Candy Sue always did what she was told, but she looked bored as a broomstick doing it. Daddy taught her how to drive, and I could hear Candy Sue laughing as she drove around the yard and down the dirt road out toward town, but when the driving lesson was over she always returned with that pout on her face and hid out in my bedroom, where she slept too much and wrote more letters to that Scott boy.

One Friday morning in late July when my daddy was at work and my mama had taken the twins to the doctor for their check-up, Candy Sue sprang up from her bed, where she had been sleeping, and rushed to the bathroom and vomited.

I had been sitting on my bed finishing up my book, *The Clue in the Crumbling Wall.* I set the book down when I heard her vomiting and went and stood in the doorway.

"It's all right, I'm not sick," Candy Sue said when she realized I was behind her.

"But what's wrong? Is this your period? Are you bleeding, Candy Sue?"

Candy Sue shook her head and said, "I only wish," then she burst into tears.

I stepped into the bathroom and placed my hand on Candy Sue's hot back and said again, "What's wrong? Candy Sue?"

She cried harder, and then she blurted out the truth, the real reason she had come to stay with us.

"I'm not sick," she said to me, flushing the toilet and blowing her nose into some toilet tissue. "I'm pregnant, and your parents know all about it, so you don't have to go telling on me."

"But you're not married," I said.

"No duh." She leaned over the sink and splashed water on her face. Then she grabbed her toothbrush and brushed her teeth while I stared at her, trying to understand.

"But how can you be pregnant if you're not married? You can't get a baby if you aren't married, Candy Sue."

Candy Sue whipped around and shouted at me, "Stop saying that!" She burst into tears again and ran back to her bed and flung herself onto it, squishing her teddy bear beneath her.

I followed her and stood over the bed and said, "What did I say? What did I say wrong, Candy Sue? What's wrong?"

"They're ashamed of me," she said, her voice muffled by her pillow. "Everyone is ashamed of me. My parents sent me here because they didn't want anyone to know I was pregnant. They had to get rid of me before it started showing." She turned her head and looked up at me. Her face was red and wet. "Don't you notice the way your parents won't look at me? They talk *at* me, not *to* me. They're nice to me, and they're trying to help by teaching me stuff they think I'm going to need to know when the baby comes, but they won't even look at me."

"But maybe if you weren't always sulking. They don't like people to sulk, that's all. Why would they be ashamed of you? What did you do?"

Then Candy Sue explained to me how after you get your period you get really interested in boys and they get interested in you and your body, and you want to take off your clothes and be together, not to make babies but because you're in love.

"At least that's what the boy wants you to believe," she said, with anger in her voice. "He'll tell you he loves you so you'll make love to him, and then when you get pregnant he—he dumps you and never answers your letters. He gets on with his life like nothing ever happened, but it's not like that for the girl. You understand? My life is over. I don't get to go to parties or proms or college or anything. I'm stuck out here in this hot hellhole, hidden away so my parents don't have to be embarrassed by me in front of all their friends." Candy Sue sat up and wiped her eyes. "It's not fair," she said. "Everyone is ashamed of me, but what about Scott? Nothing happens to him. Nobody would call him a whore. Nobody would whisper mean things about him behind his back. Nothing happens to him. Nothing!" Candy Sue cried some more. She cried so much she got hiccups. I wanted to run and get Mama or Daddy to come take care of her, because I didn't know what to do except hand her lots of toilet paper to wipe her nose and eyes with. I wished they were home.

Finally she looked up at me and said, "You notice your parents never tell *me* to practice the piano. No! That part of my life is over. I'm supposed to just stay with the babies. That's all I'm allowed to do the rest of my miserable life."

"But Candy Sue, you don't play the piano."

Candy Sue glared at me and then shouted, "Who says? You think you're so good at the piano? When I was your age I had been playing for only two years, and I was already better than my teacher. I was playing stuff most people don't learn to play for years and years. I was going to go to Juilliard. You know what that is?"

I shook my head.

"It's a world-famous school for great musicians, and I was going to go. But now that's all over. Now I'm going to be just like your mother, sweating and slaving all day over some screaming hot baby that won't shut up. The twins never stop crying. If my baby is like that I swear I'll throw it through the window!" Candy Sue picked up her teddy bear and threw it toward the bedroom window. It hit the chest of drawers and landed on the floor.

I drew in my breath. "No, you wouldn't. You would never do that, Candy Sue."

Candy Sue scowled and held her head down. "I would. I hate this baby!" Then she jumped up and ran to the window and stood in front of it, panting.

I didn't know what to say. I wanted my mama to come home. Finally I said, "Could you play me something, Candy Sue? Could you play me something on the piano and show me how good you are?"

I had hoped to distract her and I thought it had worked. She stopped crying and nodded her head. Then she turned and walked out of the room. I followed her down the hallway and down the stairs to the living room. She went over to the piano and sat down, and I stood beside her leaning on the piano. She closed her eyes a minute, and then when she opened them she said, "I'll play you Schubert's Impromptu in A-flat, Opus 90, Number 4. I know that one really well; I played it just over a month ago at my last recital." Candy Sue sniffed and wiped some lingering tears off her cheek with the back of her hand, and then after a few practice scales, which already sounded better than anything I could do, she began to play.

I had played Schubert before, but I realized as soon as I heard her play that my piece was for a beginner. Candy Sue's was the real thing. She placed her fingers on the keys and played, and it was like listening to water trickling and flowing down a stream. It was so smooth and fluid, and her hands moved all over the keyboard, her fingers so long and graceful compared to my stubby little hands. I had never heard anyone play like her before except on a record player.

She played most of it with her eyes closed. Tears leaked from beneath her lashes and spilled down her face, dropping onto the keyboard. She kept playing her beautiful music, and then her eyes opened and she stopped, and for a minute she stared down at her hands. Then she got up and headed back upstairs toward the bedroom.

"Candy Sue, why did you stop? Did you forget how to play the rest?" I asked, following her. "That was the prettiest thing I ever heard. You're so good. I hope I can play like you someday. Do you think I can play like you someday? Candy Sue?" I trotted down the hallway after her. The closer we got to the bedroom, the faster she walked. "Candy Sue, do you think I can play like you someday?"

Candy Sue didn't answer me. She strode into the bedroom and over to the closet. She pulled out my good Sunday going-to-church dress and yanked it off the hanger.

"Hey!" I shouted. "What did you do that for?"

She still didn't answer me. She took the hanger and went to the bathroom with it. When she got to the door, she turned around and said, "I'll only be a few minutes." She smiled and reached out and patted my hand. "Then I'll teach you how to play some of that Schubert, okay? Would you like that?"

I nodded.

"You go on down then and practice some scales so you'll be warmed up when I come down."

"But what are you doing?" I asked. "What are you going to do with my hanger?"

"Go on," she said, giving me a little shove. Then she closed the door and locked it.

I waited a minute by the door listening and Candy Sue called out, "Go on now. I won't teach you if you aren't warmed up."

I left. I left her upstairs in the bathroom and did just as she had asked me to do. I went down and practiced my scales, stopping every once in a while to listen, waiting for Candy Sue to come down. I practiced for a long, long time. One time I thought I heard her calling me. I stopped and listened again. I stood up and went to the bottom of the steps and listened, but I didn't hear anything. I called up to her, but she didn't answer. I started up the stairs and then I heard my mama and the twins come in the house. I ran to my mother, feeling suddenly frightened.

"Mama," I said, and then I cried, tucking my head down and pressing it against her stomach.

Mama placed her hand on my head and said, "Baby, what is it? Where's Candy Sue?"

I lifted my head and told my mama she had locked herself in the bathroom. "She said she would only be a few minutes, but it's been a long time."

"She's probably just a little sick. Why don't I go see?" Mama patted my shoulder and told me to stay with the twins. Then she started for the stairs. I followed her to the hallway and called after her, "She took a hanger in there with her, Mama."

"Oh, Lord have mercy!" Mama ran up the steps and called out to Candy Sue, but she didn't answer. Mama called again and I heard her run down the hallway toward the bathroom. I set the twins in the baby carriage that sat in the foyer and hurried up the steps to see what was wrong. When I got up there, Mama was at the bathroom door, jiggling the handle and calling out for Candy Sue to answer her. Then when Mama saw me she said, "Baby, I want you to run and get Mrs. Brambley and tell her it's an emergency, and then I want you to stay downstairs and don't you come up, you hear me?"

I nodded and then turned and ran. I ran out of the house to get Mrs. Brambley, but I knew in my heart it was too late. I knew Candy Sue was dead. I didn't know what she had done, how it had happened, until later when the medics came and took her away in an ambulance. Then I saw all the blood in the bathroom. I wasn't supposed to see anything. Mama had told me to stay with the twins, but after the medics took Candy Sue outside and Mama and Mrs. Brambley followed the stretcher out to the ambulance, I ran upstairs and I saw all the blood—the baby-making blood. I believed it was five days' worth of period blood come all at once. I stood frozen in the doorway of the bathroom, unable to look away, until Mama returned and found me standing there. She grabbed my shoulders and turned me around. Mrs. Brambley was standing behind her with a look of pity in her eyes.

"Baby, I told you to stay with the twins. Now you go on and let us clean up this mess, you hear?"

I nodded, but I didn't leave. I couldn't. I felt I belonged right there, with Mama and Mrs. Brambley. I stayed and watched them on their hands and knees cleaning up Candy Sue's blood, and Mama gave up on trying to shoo me away. They were in too much of a hurry to get everything done before my daddy got home.

When Mama and Mrs. Brambly had finished, they sighed and sat back on their heels with wet diapers used as rags clasped in their red hands. Then Mama, remembering me, looked up and told me not to tell my daddy what I had seen. She made me promise, and through my tears and sniffles I promised. Then I wiped my eyes with my arm and said, "But aren't you going to tell Daddy that she's gone? Won't he know?"

Mama nodded. "Yes, baby, he'll know, but he doesn't have to know about this." She pointed down at the freshly scoured bathroom floor. "This is women's business. It's just between us women, you understand?"

I nodded as if I understood, and in a way I did. I knew that I had just gained entrance into a secret club, a women's-only club, a club whose membership I didn't want, not then, and not ever.

Mama and Mrs. Brambley had scoured the bathroom floor good, but they didn't get all of the blood. They missed some spots underneath the sink, spots that had dried and turned to a brownish red—a maroon. I never told anyone that they were there, and every time I used the bathroom, I would stare down at the maroon spots and remember Candy Sue and the way she had died, and I vowed to myself that I would do whatever it took to keep from getting my period, even if it meant starving myself so I wouldn't get fat and my boobs wouldn't grow.

Then, after four long years of keeping my promise, while I was in the hospital for the third time getting fattened up with the nurses' forced feedings, it happened. I went to the bathroom, and there in my underpants I saw it—a spot of maroon the size of a penny—and I screamed. I shut my eyes and I screamed and screamed, and even though my eyes were closed, I could not shut out the maroon. It was everywhere, flooding the bathroom, spilling out into the hallway, waves and waves of maroon rushing down the stairwells and exploding into the lobby of the hospital and slamming against the emergency exit doors. I could still see it even when the nurse rushed into the bathroom and scooped me off the floor and held me close. There was so much blood, so much maroon. I kept screaming and howling that I was bleeding to death, and even after the nurse made me open my eyes and showed me that I hadn't bled to death at all, and promised me that I wouldn't, assuring me that my period was a sign of life and starvation was the way to death, I kept howling, howling this time for the loss of Candy Sue and the loss of my childhood.

ritual purity
by Deborah Heiligman

i'm standing in the hot sun outside this stupid liquor store, waiting for a guy who said he'd buy me a bottle. It took me like ten minutes to find someone who would do it for me, and the guy I got, he is so sceevy, I'm afraid he's going to make me pay for it in another way. I said to get me the biggest bottle of booze you can for ten dollars; I'm not used to New York prices, so I have no idea what ten dollars can get me. Probably some horrible rot gut wine, but man, I'm desperate. So I'm standing here, feeling kind of lousy about it all, when I see my aunt. She looks pretty much like all the other women of her kind here in Brooklyn: long dark skirt, stockings, long-sleeved blouse—today it's blue-and-white striped—buttoned all the way up, even though it's like ninety degrees out. But I know it's her. For one thing, she doesn't wear a wig like the other ladies. She has this whole collection of scarves she wears, and today she's wearing one that's bright blue. She looks ridiculous. For another thing, after living with her for two weeks, she has become so familiar, her face, her dark blue eyes that don't miss a thing, the way she holds her head at a tilt when she's concentrating—what is it they say? Familiarity breeds contempt? Yup. And here she is walking toward me, briskly, head tilted, with this look of determination or something on her face.

Damn her. How did she know I was here?

She told me she was going to be gone for a couple of hours, told me I should clean up after breakfast and do some laundry. Yeah right. She dropped the littlest boys at a baby-sitter—she sure doesn't trust me to take care of them—so I made my escape. What does she think I am, an effing maid? Like hell. In fact I told her to go to hell, and she told me Jews don't believe in hell, really. Hell for Jews is no fire and brimstone. It's more like a bad neighborhood.

Like this one. This stinking neighborhood, with half the people like her and half the people from countries I've never even heard of. It's hell enough for me.

Which was, I guess, exactly the point.

I quickly turn toward the liquor store, press the side

of my face up to the dirty bricks, and pray like mad she hasn't seen me yet. It's not that I can't handle her, I can, but I just don't feel like it. And then, just as she is getting so close to me that I can hear her heels click, click, click on the sidewalk, and I can smell her perfume—Charlie, I think it is, the same damn kind my mother wore—the guy comes out, shoves the brown paper bag in my hand, and leaves.

I'm ready for her now, armed with my booze, but she keeps walking.

Does she see me and ignore me? Or is she so much in her own little world that she tunes out everyone and everything on this street that isn't part of Orthodox Jewland? That's not like her. This lady does not miss a damn thing.

So what is she up to? If she wasn't coming for me, what is she doing? I get all kinds of crazy ideas. She's going to the police to turn me in. She's having an affair. She's going to the doctor because she's dying of cancer and she hasn't told anyone yet. My heart beats a little faster.

I can't help myself, I follow her. I trail her about a half a block behind, weaving in and out of religious Jews talking in Yiddish, all kinds of moms pushing strollers, the religious ones with double strollers that take up the whole sidewalk, and guys hanging out, leering at me. I have to watch out for piles of dog shit and garbage, too. It stinks, this place; it's not at all like my little white-bread hometown in Pennsylvania, which I hated, of course. Meanwhile I'm clutching my paper bag, and I still have no idea what the guy bought me.

All of a sudden she stops, looks around a little, kind of secretly, and turns into an alley. I'm close now, so I stand against a building and peer around the wall into the alley. She kind of ducks her head, as if she doesn't want anyone to see what she's doing, and then she goes into the side door of an old stone building.

It's true! She's having an affair. I love it! See, I knew she was a fake. Wearing a scarf instead of a wig. Like she's one of them, but not. And she talks like them, in Yiddish and stuff, as if she came off the boat about a century ago, but I know she grew up with my mother in the 1970s in goddamn Pennsylvania. I knew she wasn't really one of them! She's a goddamn phony.

I walk to the front of the building to see what it is—is she meeting someone at his apartment or at his office, or what? This is too cool. I've got blackmail possibilities! Moishe being a hotshot lawyer and all—he couldn't afford to let the public know his religious wife was stepping out on him. Oh yeah. I could blackmail both of them and use the dough to get the hell out of here. But then I see fucking Hebrew letters above the door. And a brass plaque that says Brooklyn Mikveh.

It is some stupid Jewish thing. Of course. I don't know what a *mikveh* is, but it sure as hell isn't something in the real world. I go into the alley where she turned, lean against the damp bricks, and take the bottle out of the bag. Shit, it's some horrible peach wine, a chardonnay. It's supposed to be cold, but what can I do? Thank God it has a twist cap. I open it up, and take myself a huge swig. It tastes like crap, but once it hits, it feels like my salvation.

When I walk into the kitchen the next morning, I feel horrible. My head is throbbing like I drank a whole bottle of rot gut. Oh yeah, I did. Coffee. Give me coffee. I need coffee. Ouch. Those brats need to stop screaming. Why are they always screaming? And not just in English, but in Yiddish and Hebrew, too.

I'm still not even sure how many of them there are. They all look alike, especially the older ones, in their stupid dark pants, white shirts, and those dumb yarmulkes. Avi, Yitzi, Schmitzi, Fitzi. No, probably not Schmitzi and Fitzi.

Coffee.

I find my way through the throngs to the pot and pour myself a cup. At least the aliens make good coffee. It's Moishe's doing. He gets these really good beans from Manhattan and then grinds them fresh every morning. It's like a religion with him, but one I can get into.

I leave before anyone can bother me, and plop myself on the rotten old couch in the living room. It crunches from cereal and crackers when I land.

This house is such a mess. At home my father keeps everything so neat and tidy I'm not even sure we live there.

So how many are there? They're always running around and yelling, so I can't count them. I feel like there are ten of them. But maybe there are only four. Only! After six years of just me and my father, Silent Larry, anything more than two would seem like a lot. Well, if I'm gonna stay here I guess I'd better get them straight.

Oh, oops. Earth to Mimi. You are *not* staying the whole hot stinky summer here. How I thought I could spend a summer in Brooklyn with these freaks—

Ah, but it wasn't exactly my idea. My dear father turns me in and then tells me I gotta go to some horrible boot camp for troubled kids. If I were eighteen, he would have put me in jail. The only reason I'm here is because of The Aunt. He called her to moan about me, and she said she would not have me going off to some horrible place where I'd meet people worse than I was. That's what she said. So Larry worked out this deal with the cops. Still, I gotta say it surprises me that Barbara would let me come here and be around her boys if I'm so bad. But I'm guessing she thinks she has The Power to Turn Me Around. So here I am, bad girl Mimi, in Orthodox Jewland, surrounded by religious freak Aunt Barbara, her nerdy husband, Moishe, who is definitely from another planet, and this mass of horrible little boys. . . .

I reach into my bathrobe pocket and grab a couple of pills. I gulp them down with my last sip of coffee. They'll get me through one more day.

Aunt Barbara comes in and says something to me, but I ignore her. If I talk, even a little, she considers it an

invitation and pounds me with questions and harangues.
"What were you thinking with all those drugs?" and "Two
boys, you were with *two* boys at once?" and "Your dear
mother, may she rest in peace, you would have killed her
if she weren't already dead." So I have learned not to give
Barbara the opportunity.

"Well, will you?"

"Will I what?"

"Will you help me cook today? Tonight is the Sabbath,
and I have a lot to do."

Uh, no. I get up, walk past her, and go back into my
bedroom to get dressed. My bedroom. Yeah, right. It's
this tiny little room on the first floor that Moishe's old
mother used to sleep in. She died a few months ago,
and I swear it still smells like old lady shit. All the other
bedrooms are upstairs, I think. It's a tiny house.
Moishe the lawyer could afford a bigger one, but I bet
it's too important for them to stay in this crummy
neighborhood. I gotta get out of here. I put on the stupid
long skirt and long-sleeved shirt Barbara makes me
wear. But I leave my blouse unbuttoned below my bra.
I'm popping out all over. Hah. Serves her right. Bitch
threw out all my other clothes. Well, she can't make me

take out my earrings, my tongue stud, and my belly button ring. Those and what drugs I have left are my last connection with sanity.

I take my birth control pill. It's my last one. Should I get more? How could I? I have no doctor, no prescription. Besides, from the looks of the guys around here, the last thing in the (ha ha) fucking world I'm going to need is birth control pills. Unlike Aunt Barbara, whose method of birth control seems to be pregnancy.

I throw the empty pill container into the trash and walk down the hall. I'm getting out. Going somewhere, anywhere. I don't have much money, just the little I had and what I could steal from Larry before I left. I'm down to only like fifty bucks. But I'll find something to do.

Barbara grabs my arm. Tries to button up my shirt, but I pull away. She throws something at me.

"Put it on, Miriam."

"Huh?"

"It's an apron. And I told you, it's Friday, we are having company, and I need your help cooking. You've been here for weeks already, and you have yet to pick up a finger in this house. Today you are helping me."

"My name is Mimi, not Miriam. And I'm not helping."

"You want me to call your father? Tell him about the booze and the pills? He'll get here in two hours and take you to that juvenile detention camp."

No way out.

"Why do you wear that stupid scarf on your head? And why don't you wear a wig like the other ladies?" I learned this from fighting with my dad: The best defense is a good offense.

"It's part of our rules, Miriam. Married women cover their hair. I do wear a wig sometimes, to shul— synogogue—or when I'm really dressing up. But the scarves are more comfortable, and more *me*. And it's fine, as long as I cover my hair, because women's hair is so distracting to men. Only Moishe can see my hair."

"Like your hair is so beautiful it's gonna give the UPS man a hard-on?"

I am really disgusted by this whole thing. I looked up on the Internet—they let me use their computer at night—what a *mikveh* is. It's a place, a bath kind of thing, where women go when their periods are over so they can have sex with their husbands. Part of the laws of what they call "ritual purity." It's just disgusting. But it said that even guys go there, on Fridays before sundown, to "mark a distinction between the regular every day week and the holy Sabbath." And people go to the *mikveh* when they convert to Judaism. To wash away their pasts, I guess.

"Eat something, Miriam," Aunt Barbara says. "We've got a lot of cooking to do. Eat." She's already started taking measuring cups and stuff out of the cupboard and somehow has gotten flour on her nose. She looks funny.

"I don't eat in the morning," I tell her for the billionth time, although I am feeling surprisingly hungry. The eggs she made for the boys must have gotten my stomach acids going.

"You hung over?"

"Leave me alone or—"

"Look, let's call a truce. Let me teach you how to make challah today. Do you remember the time I came to visit and we made challah? You were about ten, I think."

I shake my head no. I might remember, but then again, I might not. I open the fridge and grab the milk. I'm not even sure it's okay for me to have something with milk right now. You gotta keep milk and meat separate in this house. But she doesn't say anything, so I get the cereal and go to what I hope is the dairy cupboard and grab a bowl. I hold up the bowl and shrug my shoulders.

"Yes, that's fine."

"Good, because I sure wouldn't want to—God forbid—*use the wrong bowl*," I say sarcastically. I don't want her to think I'm buying the party line.

"Sure you remember," she says, ignoring me. "I was visiting for the weekend. I taught you and your mother how to make challah. Then we went swimming?"

"Yeah, I remember." Oh damn, I made her smile. I want to take it back, but I really do remember that visit.

"You used to hold your breath so long underwater it drove your mother crazy."

I nod. I remember that, too.

"And you did a belly flop off the diving board, and it hurt so much. Remember? You cried and cried. Your mom and I, we wrapped you in a towel and hugged you for about an hour."

After I had stopped bawling, we went home and baked the challahs. The three of us ate one whole loaf right out of the oven. Hot, soft, a little sweet. Man, that was the best bread I had ever tasted. But I'm not telling her that.

Her eyes are filling with tears. Not the whole I-miss-my-sister-Elaine crying thing, I hope. I can't deal with it. I give her a dirty look.

"C'mon," she says, shaking her head. "Let me show you how we do this."

She mixes up flour and salt and sugar and yeast and oil and eggs, in a big bowl. I eat my cereal and I don't pay too much attention, anyway, because I'm not staying here. But then Barbara takes my hands and places them in the mound of dough.

"You knead with the heels of your hands. First you push the dough away from you. Go ahead, push it away. Now pull it back, make it into a mound again. Push away, pull back, push away, pull back. You can pound it a bit; it will survive."

I knead and knead, pushing away, pulling back, mounding it into a ball, and starting over. It stops being a sticky mess and starts to become something. A shape, a form, a whole. And it feels so good in my hands, so smooth. Sensual, kinda. And it's like, I don't know, like I can take out all my feelings on this mound of dough, and it's okay. It's what I'm supposed to be doing.

"Does it feel elastic?" she asks me.

"I don't know."

"Poke it with your finger. If it springs back, it's ready."

It's ready. Barbara takes it, puts it into a big white bowl, covers it with a damp towel, and puts it on the counter where the sun is shining. I never even noticed that any sun came into this room, but there it is, shining on the challah dough.

"What do you remember about your mother?" she asks me as we're cleaning up.

"Nothing."

"Try to remember. . . ."

"I don't remember, and I don't care, Barbara. About my dead mother, about challah, about you, about any of it. Please leave me alone."

Truth is, I am actually desperate for more information about Mom. My father never talks about her. But there's no way am I going to let Barbara know that, this person who grew up in a normal house and became a freak who doesn't have sex with her husband for two weeks out of the month. I read that, too, on the Internet. They can't touch while she's bleeding, or for a week after. Not even to pass the salt.

Barbara starts making other things while the challahs rise: roasted chicken, carrot tsimis. I try to leave, but she keeps giving me things to do: peel carrots, measure sugar, mash garlic, season chicken. The kitchen starts to smell delicious. Larry's idea of a home-cooked meal is bagged salad and boxed macaroni and cheese.

The phone rings. Barbara answers it. Her face gets that look on it—I know the look already. It's Larry. "It's your father, Miriam," she says. "He wants to talk to you before the Sabbath."

I shake my head no as I have every time he's called. Which has been a lot more often than I would have thought.

"Please, Miriam, for *shalom bayis*, peace in the house."

"I'm not in his house anymore, remember? He kicked me out!"

Barbara shakes her head, frowns at me with disapproval. Raises her eyebrows in a question, but I shake my head and turn away.

"Larry, she's helping me cook and she can't get away just now."

How lame. She listens for a few minutes, makes reassuring sounds, says "she's fine" about fifty times, and hangs up.

"He's worried about you," she says.

"Like hell," is what I say. It's about time, is what I think.

Barbara turns away from me, and I hear her mumbling. Is she counting to ten or saying a prayer?

She uncovers the dough and nods. "The dough is done rising," she says to me. "You give it a good punch, smack it, hard."

I smack it with all my might. I can't help it. It feels so good. Once, twice, three times. Four times. It's Larry. My mother. This lady. My stupid self.

"Okay, I think we've got a new kind of therapy; we are going to be rich!" Barbara laughs.

I punch some more, harder, and finally Barbara puts her hand on my arm. "We're not trying to kill it, *bubbeleh*." She takes the dough from me. "Now we have to braid it."

First she separates the dough into three loaves. Then for each loaf we roll out four long snakes of dough. "Connect the four strands at one end, then you go from the left over two, under one, and from the right, over two, under one. . . ."

She looks so content. How can that be? All she does all day is take care of kids, cook, clean, pray. But she's happy. Man, I can't remember the last time I was happy.

"Now we let the loaves rise again, and before we put them in the oven to bake, we'll paint them with beaten egg to make them shiny and put seeds on them. What kind of seeds do you like? Poppy or sesame?"

"Both."

"Just like your mother," she says, and smiles at me. "May she rest in peace."

And all of a sudden it's too much. I hate her, I hate her being nice to me. I hate her for trying to bring back my mother.

"My mother? My *mother*!" I say it like a curse. "An idiot who goes and dies when you are eleven, without any warning, and then six months later you get your period, and you have no idea what to do because your stupid-ass father is still walking around like the truck hit him, not her . . . and all that blood covering your bed and your underpants for days because you don't have the nerve to ask him to go get you something—well, I don't want to talk about my mother anymore, ever. I hate her and I hate you."

I turn to go, to run to my room for more pills, but Barbara grabs my arms and puts her face right up close to mine. She is red as anything. "Don't you ever, ever say that again. You should be ashamed of yourself. Your mother would be so ashamed of you. I am so glad she's not alive to see you, to see how you've turned out."

I wrench myself away from her and run to my room. "I haven't turned out yet," I scream, but I hear the door slam. She has run out of the house.

I think I'm going to take a million pills, but instead I collapse onto my bed and sob. And sob. And sob. Until I have nothing left inside me. And then I sleep.

A knock on the door wakes me up.

"Go away," I say.

"I want to talk to you," Aunt Barbara says. "I was stupid. Wrong. I'm sorry."

I don't say anything.

"I'm polishing silver. Come help, if you want. It's good therapy too."

Silver, huh? That I could pawn, or sell. Raise enough

cash to take a bus to Florida or something.

She's at the dining room table, surrounded by tons of silver. Candlesticks and stuff. It was my grandmother's. She told me that the first Sabbath I was here.

I take a cloth and grab a big water pitcher to polish. It's round and curved, and has an intricate design of flowers on the front. The crevices are filled with tarnish. I get the main part gleaming and then go at the design with a toothbrush, and before I can stop myself, I hear my own voice telling her that I'm sorry.

"I don't hate her, you know." I miss her every single goddamn day.

"Oh, Miriam, I am so sorry I said that to you, about your mother being ashamed. You would never have turned out—things would have been different if she hadn't died. Really different."

"Tell me about it."

"I will tell you about it. What it's been like for me. Maybe someday you will tell me more about what it has been like for you."

I start rubbing a silver serving dish really hard. It's got a tree etched into it, and I am going to get the tarnish out of there, too.

"That's an *aitz chaim*, a tree of life," she says, nodding at the dish. Before I can think of a smart-assed retort—I'm still myself, just a little sorry—she continues. "Your mother's death is what made me move here, come into this world," Aunt Barbara says. "Or what pushed me into the final decision."

I knew she and Mom hadn't grown up as Orthodox Jews. They had grown up as regular Jews, going to Temple sometimes, but no big deal. And my mother had married a non-Jew, and that was cool with her parents.

"So?"

"I met Moishe in college. We got to know each other arguing. I was an atheist, he was an Orthodox Jew. The more we argued, the more we talked, the more time we spent together. He was—is—brilliant, and funny, and passionate. And so we fell in love." She blushes. Jeez. And shrugs. "But if your mother hadn't died, I don't know if I would have married him."

"Why?"

"Do you remember I came to stay with you for a while after the funeral?"

I nodded. I do remember. I clung to Aunt Barbara every minute. She felt like Mom, smelled like Mom. Is that when she started wearing the same perfume as Mom? I kind of remember her doing that, going to Mom's dresser and spraying it on. I'll have to ask her someday.

"Your father wanted me to leave. I think I reminded him too much of her. And I was just someone else for him to take care of. I was a mess. She was my best friend. So I went back to school and told Moishe I would marry him."

"Because you loved him, or because you were running away?"

"*Touché.* I did love him. But I think I was also—not running away, but looking for something. I needed something from this life. The rules, the rituals, the comfort. And the faith. I had to make sense of a senseless world. . . ."

"And?"

"And what?"

"Does it make sense?"

"It does. I know it's not right for everyone—"

"It's not for me, that's for sure."

"I know," says Barbara. "I know this isn't right for you." She looks like she wants to say more, but she doesn't.

I can fill it in: Neither is popping pills, getting drunk, and sleeping with every guy I meet.

One morning after breakfast, the older boys have gone off to their Yeshiva camp thing and Barbara asks me to watch the twins while she takes a shower. It turns out there are five little boys, and the two youngest, the toddlers, are twins. Who knew? It only took me like six weeks to figure that out! So I'm sitting there with the boys, and I've got both of them on my lap. We're watching *Dora the Explorer*, this little kids' show they love.

They smell so good, these little guys, of baby shampoo, and bananas or something. On Fridays they smell like challah. While they watch the show, one of them plays with my hair. The other one thinks he's put his thumb in his mouth, but it's my thumb. I gently take it out and find his thumb for him and give him a little tickle. He snuggles up against me, and for one brief moment I am happy.

Dora is asking for help, and the boys are shouting back to the TV, "Close the gate," when I hear someone else shouting. It takes me a couple of minutes to realize it's Barbara. "Miriam, help me!" she's yelling.

I quickly put the babies in the playpen and run down the hall.

"Where are you?" I yell, and then I hear a thud in the bathroom.

I push open the door, and I see her lying on the floor.

There is blood everywhere, all over the toilet and the floor. And all over Aunt Barbara. She is wrapped in her towel, barely, and there is blood coming from down there. It is weird what I think at that moment, I can't help it: She looks so much more like my mother than I realized. It's the hair. I see her hair down for the first time, and it's Mom's hair. It's gorgeous. No wonder she rarely stuffs it into a wig. It is long, dark, dark black, beautifully wavy, and it is cascading over the white tile floor. Black, white, red.

"Help me," she moans.

I stare at her stupidly. What am I supposed to do? "What happened?" I ask.

"A miscarriage." I didn't even know she was pregnant.

I run out of the bathroom, my heart is pounding. I keep seeing the blood.

My hands reach for the pills I always keep in my pocket, my secret emergency stash. They are painkillers. They would give me a real nice high. I hold them in my hand.

I check on the babies; they're fine in the playpen, watching TV.

I grab the cordless phone and call 911 as I rush back to the bathroom. She is moaning, holding her stomach, and crying as they answer. I give them the address, tell them "miscarriage," and ask if I can give her some of these pills. They tell me I can't.

"I was hoping my drugs would come in handy, but they said no." She smiles a weak smile, but I can tell she's really hurting.

And damn it, I can't help her.

She starts to talk, to tell me what to do, but I shush her, put a rolled-up towel under her head, and run to the kitchen to get Moishe's phone number from the refrigerator.

I am an emergency machine. I call him and make his secretary break into a meeting he's having with a client. He asks me how much blood there is and I tell him a lot. I hang up and call next door, tell the neighbor to come get the twins. The minute I hang up with her, Moishe calls back, starts to give me instructions. I interrupt him. My voice is shaky, but I try to make it sound strong. "Meet us at the hospital. I'm going with her. The ambulance is here." And I hang up.

Nothing like a crisis to turn you into a person, I guess.

In the next weeks, I, bad Mimi, learn how to run a house and take care of kids. At first, of course, Moishe doesn't trust me worth shit, and he brings in an old religious aunt of his to do it all. In a couple of days, though, we all realize that I can do it better than she can. We get along okay, I'm not a bitch to her or anything, but I am the one who knows where everything is, and I am the one the kids go to when they need something. The little guys follow me everywhere. I have to peel them off me to go to the bathroom.

And I am the one Aunt Barbara wants to help her to the bathroom in the beginning. And I am the one Barbara wants to talk to when she gets depressed. Turns out the miscarriage itself wasn't so bad. It was very early on. The doctor said there's often a lot of blood, even so.

But Barbara feels like it was her fault.

"I must have done something wrong," she cries to me one afternoon, after I put the twins down for their nap. "All these boys and I can't hold in a girl."

"It was a girl?"

Barbara nods but can't talk.

I hold her while she cries, and remind her the doctor said she could try again soon.

"I would have named her after your mother," she says.

"I know."

That evening Larry calls again. This time I talk to him. Tell him that Barbara is getting better. I even tell him a funny story about the boys and Moishe, how they all got dressed up in superhero costumes and put on a show for us the other night. Barbara laughed and laughed. Especially when Moishe started jumping off the bed and calling himself SuperNerd. "Ya gotta like the guy," I tell my father. It's a jab, but I can't help it.

"I always did," he says to me.

I can't say that I forgive Larry completely, for being so damn out of it, but I understand him a little more. I mean, I know how I felt when I saw Barbara lying on the floor in all that blood. Imagine him seeing my mother all wrecked up in the hospital and having to take her off life support and everything. Forget about it. He deserved a year or two of walking around like a zombie. Not really his fault that by the time he came out of it, I was already in it neck deep.

Thing is, I am thinking all these things, and I am acting like a person who knows what's up, but inside I still want to take pills and drink booze and be bad.

And then, nature's (or God's?) little way of testing me, I guess: I get really bad PMS, which I'd only heard about, never had before. I cry and yell and bitch for a week. And then, when I finally get my period after not having it all summer, I guess from going off the pill and all the stress, I am so damned crampy, I really, really want to take drugs. Major drugs. But in a fit of guilt or anger or something, while Barbara was in the hospital I had flushed them all down the toilet. And Barbara finished all her good painkillers, and all she has in the house is Midol and stuff like that. So I have to deal. I sit with the kids and a heating pad on my lap for about two days straight, bleeding and cramping, and feeling like shit. And that's when I know what I have to do and why I ask Barbara for her help.

•

After dinner, a few days after my period is over, Barbara comes into my room. "Are you done?"

"Yes," I say.

"Completely done?"

"I guess."

"Go check."

"How?"

"Stick a tampon in and see if any blood is on it. No, bring it to me and I'll look at it."

"What? You crazy? I'm not going to—"

"Miriam, you asked for this—"

"Okay, okay."

I go into the bathroom and come back, holding a tampon by the string. "This is so gross."

Barbara clicks her tongue and looks closely at the tampon. "Okay. It's clean. We'll go tonight after the boys are asleep. If you're ready, that is."

I am more than ready. For the last month, while I took care of Barbara and the boys, all I did was think of everything bad and stupid and self-destructive I have done for the past five years.

I nod my head. "So what do I do?"

"You need to cut your nails, clean them out completely, no dirt can be left. Fingers and toes. Take a shower, wash everything very well, two, three times, including your hair. Take off your nail polish. Take out all your earrings, all fifty million of them, your tongue stud, your belly button ring—"

"But why?"

"The water has to go into every pore of your body to purify you. Nothing can get in the way. Not even a little piece of lint."

"Okay."

"You can always put them back in." But somehow I know I won't.

"What else?"

"That's all. You leave the rest to me."

We're in the alley, breaking into the *mikveh*. I can't believe it. It must be about midnight. No one is around.

"Why did you go in this door that other time, not the front door?"

She raises her eyebrow in a question, but passes over it. I guess she didn't see me that day. "It's a matter of privacy. Nobody has to know a woman's business."

"Huh. How did you get the key for tonight?"

"The *mikveh* lady's son owes Moishe a favor. He made some drug charges disappear. He got it for me."

"Wow." Moishe's in on this. I can't believe it. I'm not supposed to go to the *mikveh*, according to the Orthodox Jews. Because I'm not married. I'm not converting or anything. So Barbara is sort of breaking the rules for me. With Moishe's help. I love it.

"I don't want to turn on any lights, so we are going to have to walk slowly. I'll lead the way."

She holds my hand, steers me down darkened hallways, into a kind of small locker room.

"Take off your clothes."

"Gee the last time somebody said that to me it was a guy and he was already naked and . . ." I feel Barbara stiffen. "I'm sorry, I'm just nervous. I had to go for the joke."

"It's okay."

My eyes are getting used to the dark and I can see Barbara smiling a little.

"Are you coming in too?" I say, taking off my underwear.

"No, sweetheart, this is just for you. I'll be right next to you, though."

I almost tell her not to call me sweetheart. But I don't.

She unlocks another door and there it is, the *mikveh*. Barbara brought a flashlight, and in here she turns it on so we can see. The *mikveh* itself is just like a little pool, tiled and everything. You have to walk down steps to get into it. "One of the things that makes a *mikveh* a *mikveh*," she tells me, "is that you have to have fresh water running into it. So they collect rainwater in a cistern, and then we turn this tap and the fresh water flows in and mixes with the other water."

"It has to be living water," I say.

"Yes. How do you know?"

"I looked it up."

She smiles.

"Are we doing it the way you do it, and the other Orthodox ladies?"

"No, we're doing something just for you. Do you trust me?"

"Yes."

"Okay. Then do everything I say."

I walk down the steps into water. It is not hot, not cold. Warm, like the babies' bath.

"You are going to immerse yourself completely. But before you do, I want you to think of all the things you have done in your life that you want to wash away."

"How long we got?"

"As long as you need." I was joking, but Barbara is serious.

"When you are ready, I want you to say out loud what you want to wash away. Your sins. You can whisper them to yourself. This is not for me. This is for you."

"I want you to listen," I say.

"Okay."

"Bad sex, drugs, stealing, lying, drinking, doing lousy in school, being mean to my father. . . ."

I stop. I am done.

I look at Barbara. My eyes have gotten used to the dim light, and I know her well enough now to know that she thinks I am not done. She's tilting her head in that way she has when she's thinking hard. And I know what she is thinking. "It's not a sin, really."

She just looks at me.

I don't know if I can say it. Finally, the words come. "Forgetting my mother."

"And?"

"Losing myself."

Barbara leans over and gives me a kiss on my head.

"Okay. If you're ready, go ahead."

I take a deep breath and go under. I don't want to scare Barbara, but I hold my breath and hold it and hold it. I want so much to wash away my past. I know I have to before I can figure out my future.

I know I can't go back home. I want to make peace with my father. I do. But I want to live here. For a while. Not to become Orthodox, I don't think, but to put myself back together. I don't know exactly what I want, but I know what I don't want—to go backward.

And most of all, I want to be near Barbara.

I come up, out of the water, gasping.

"Oh, thank God! I was scared," Barbara shouts. She reaches down, pulls me up out of the water, wraps a towel around me, and hugs me hard. "Mimi! I thought you weren't coming back up!"

"I'm not Mimi," I tell her. "My name is Miriam."

losing it

by Julie Stockler

the first time Jessie saw the Northern Lights, she was lying beneath a Texan guy she didn't know on a stony beach in Wawa, Ontario.

A hole-in-the-wall along the northeastern shores of Lake Superior, Wawa was a legendary stop in that favorite summertime sport of young American hippies known as "hitching across Canada, man." Jessie fantasized about hitching through Canada the way her mother dreamed about going on a cruise. She would get a flannel sleeping bag from the local Army Navy surplus store, strap it with old leather belts to the steel frame of a backpack, and hit the side of the highway with a red bandana reining in her long brown curls. She would cock her thumb toward Canada, and before long, a Volkswagen microbus with a peace sign bumper sticker would roll to a stop. The side door would slide open, and a bearded guy with a harmonica in one hand would lean out.

"Hey, man, we're headed to Thunder Bay, Ontario," he'd say. "Gonna check out the commune scene up there."

"Far out," she'd reply and crawl across the brown shag carpeting. She'd find a place to curl up among the tribe of guys and girls wearing tattered jeans, T-shirts or embroidered work shirts, and brown leather sandals. Sometimes the daydream even included a bouncy black Labrador retriever named Hendrix, who also wore a red bandana around his neck and carried a yellow Frisbee in his mouth.

There was only one problem with the whole scenario: Jessie was seventeen and she wasn't allowed to hitchhike.

"How should I know why?" Jessie said to Marlene as she poured over her dad's roadmap of Canada on her bed one Friday night in May. "They just give me one of those stupid speeches that start with 'you're a young girl' and end with 'mass murderers.'"

The two friends were lying across Jessie's purple bedspread amid a zoo of stuffed dogs and teddy bears. Carole sprawled on her belly on the floor, curling her bare toes in and out of the lavender wall-to-wall carpeting as she scribbled a letter in her spiral notebook. Ed, as always, was trawling through her collection of records, which stood like soldiers on the floor next to her stereo.

"Are you guys allowed to hitch?" Jessie asked.

"Are you kidding? They'd kill me," Marlene said, threading a needle with strands of yellow embroidery floss and setting to work stitching a daisy on the knees of her jeans.

"Me too," said Carole.

"Bummer," Ed said. He pulled out The Beatles' *White Album* from her record collection and set it on the turntable. Like most of the boys she knew, Ed's parents didn't care how he got from one place to another, as long as they didn't have to drive him or give him the car. He hitched to school, to friends' houses, even to concerts in downtown Detroit.

Boys had it made, Jessie thought. Just look at the four of them. All three girls were going to college in the fall, just like everyone expected. Carole and Marlene at least got to go out of state because their parents could afford the extra tuition. She, on the other hand, had to go to the University of Michigan in Ann Arbor, just one hour west of Southfield High. An hour! But Ed? He was going to really live life after graduation. Maybe study pottery with the elders at a Hopi reservation in Arizona, maybe learn to ride horses and work on a ranch in Wyoming. Last week, he was even talking about working on a fishing boat off the coast of Alaska and getting to know "the north country."

Jessie was determined to get to know some part of anywhere besides Southfield in that summer between graduation and college. She had heard from the guys in the bike shops that by following Highway 17, you could cycle all the way around the lake, camping anywhere you wanted for free. The four friends had been biking through the Detroit suburbs together since junior high, and the stretch of Canada forming the northern boundary of Lake Superior seemed like a realistic target.

"Look at these names. White River, Beaver Bay, Grand Portage. God, doesn't that sound incredibly beautiful?" she said, following the red highway line around the lake with her finger.

"Is 'sexual frenzy' one word or two?" asked Carole, winding her long blonde hair around and around her pen.

"You are so psychotic. I bet James Taylor gives all your letters to the FBI," said Marlene, tearing the embroidery floss with her teeth.

"I can't believe my parents are worried about me getting lost. I mean, look at this map. There's only one way around Lake Superior," Jessie said. She highlighted the road with a yellow marker.

"Yeah, well, my mom is all freaked out that I'm gonna lose something else," Carole said. She ripped the letter from the notebook, folded it into an envelope, and licked the flap.

Marlene and Jessie looked up.

"She thinks some big, fine Canadian lumberjack is going to pop out of the woods and, you know . . . deflower me."

"Cool," Ed said from the corner.

"Shut up, Ed," Jessie said. "Did you tell your mom that's the whole reason we want to take Ed? To protect our virtue."

"He'd better not protect mine," Carole said. "I mean, come on. I'm going to be eighteen in three weeks. This is getting embarrassing already."

"I thought you were saving yourself for James Taylor," said Jessie.

"I wish. Oh James, James, take me, James," Carole said, kissing the envelope with loud sucking noises.

"You are so completely gross," Marlene said. "Could we please change the subject?" She pulled the needle in and out of her jeans faster and faster. Like a sewing machine, Jessie thought.

Jessie didn't mind talking about virginity, but she had no immediate plans to lose hers. Not that she was a prude or anything. She just wanted sex to be something really, well, special. Deep. And there was no way that was going to happen with the immature boys who pimpled the halls of Southfield High, that's for sure. Jessie figured that when the time was right, she would just know it.

"Why do they call it deflower, anyway?" Carole whispered from the floor. "I mean, if you think about it, it's like the furthest thing from a flower."

"Oh gross!" they all squealed hysterically.

"What?" Ed asked. "What's so funny?"

The girls started laughing even harder.

"Okay, check this out, man. You play this song backward, and you can hear John saying it," Ed said as he rotated the record in the wrong direction with his finger. "Hear it? 'Paul is dead. Paul is dead.'"

All Jessie could hear was waves of something that sounded like Martian, with a few painful screeches where the turntable needle was grinding into the record. "Get away from my stuff, you demented freak," Jessie said, flicking her highlighter at Ed's head.

For the next three weeks, Jessie worked on the trip every hour she wasn't in school. On the weekends, she dragged Ed, Carole, and Marlene from one bike shop to another to compare prices of bicycle packs and tire repair kits; on weeknights, she set the table, made the salad, and did the dinner dishes without being asked. She kept her room clean and the short skirts her father hated in her closet. By the end of May, the plan came together. She got permission to bike around Lake Superior with her friends for two weeks, right after graduation. It wasn't hitching, but it would at least put Jessie in Canada with a sleeping bag.

The first step was an unbelievably boring twelve-hour bus ride north to Sault Sainte Marie, Michigan, which was where Canada met Michigan on Lake Superior. The four unloaded their three English and one French ten-speed bicycles, four flannel sleeping bags and new bicycle packs, two tents they'd borrowed from a cousin of Carole's, a frying pan, a pot, and a bunch of mess kits left over from Girl Scout camp. They spent the night in a local campground, pedaled their way through Canadian customs, and by 10 A.M., hit Highway 17 North.

By 11 A.M., Jesse knew she was in trouble.

"Oh, my God," Jessie said, gasping for air as she rolled her bike to a stop at a gas station that was the first sign of life she had seen since the border. It looked like those black-and-white photographs in history books on the Great Depression. There was one rusty red gas pump, a prehistoric soda machine, and a faded, painted sign that would have said OFFICE, if it wasn't missing the second f. Through the windows she could see two old men, each wearing a baseball cap and a plaid shirt. They sat on folding chairs with their feet up on an old wooden desk and didn't even look up from their newspapers as Marlene pulled up beside her, red-faced and panting.

"I'm going to die," she groaned. "I push and I push, and just when I think I've finally gotten to the top—"

"A whole new mountain comes out of nowhere. I know," Jessie said. She propped her bike against the dirty, white cinder block walls and slid to the ground.

Marlene slid down next to her, wiping a wad of dust and sweat from around her neck with her blue bandana. Jessie pulled out her map.

"Oh, my God. We've only gone four miles."

"Can a butt get blisters? I think my butt has blisters," Marlene replied.

"There's no way we're going forty miles a day," Jessie said. That's how much she figured they'd have to cycle each day in order to make it around the lake in two weeks. That wasn't going to be a problem, since she and her friends were used to biking twenty miles in an afternoon in Southfield. Then again, there wasn't a hill to be found in Southfield, or maybe even in any of the three counties that made up metropolitan Detroit.

Now that she was no longer on the bicycle seat, Jessie was suddenly aware of an uncomfortable wetness between her legs. She slammed her thighs together. Great. Her period wasn't supposed to come for another week, and she had figured on buying tampons when she needed them, instead of taking up valuable space in her pack.

"Marlene, do you have a tampon?" Jessie hissed, never taking her eyes off of the men.

"Oh gross."

"Shut up. Do you?"

"No. I'm done till we get home. Maybe there's a machine in the bathroom?"

Thankfully, the gray steel door to the bathroom wasn't locked. By pulling on the grimy chain of a single dusty lightbulb, Jessie could see that yes, there was a tampon machine. With the handle broken off.

She stuffed a wad of toilet paper into her panties and waddled out, just as Ed and Carole came into view from the highway. They were slowly walking their English racing bikes through the dusty gravel and singing at the top of their lungs.

"Follow the, follow the, follow the, follow the, follow the yellow brick road. We're off to see the wizard, the won-der-ful wiz-ard of OZZZZZZ."

Ed and Carole collapsed at the wall. Jessie bent down and whispered into Carole's ear.

"Yeah. In the front zippered pocket. In a plastic bag, at the bottom."

"Oh, my God, thank you, thank you, thank you. I love you so much."

"What?" said Ed, squeezing the very last drops of

water out of his water bottle onto his head.

"Nothing," Jessie said, as she pulled a Tampax out of Carole's pack, cupped it covertly in her fingers, and slid it all the way down into her back pocket. Even though Ed was one of her best friends, he was still a guy. And no matter how close you were, you just didn't share period stuff with a guy. She stealthily pulled out a clean pair of panties from her own pack and hit the bathroom again.

When she came out, Jessie joined Marlene, Carole, and Ed, who were now in the office chatting with the two old guys. The guy with the green hat was digging through a tackle box for Canadian change for the Coke machine. He confirmed that, yep, Highway 17 was just one endless chain of hills for the next one hundred miles or so.

"Hell," the other one said. "I'm headed up to River Bend, if a couple of you kids wanna sit with the bikes in the back of my truck, I could give you a lift up there."

From that moment on, the team began to make excellent time. They'd break camp sometime late morning and hit the side of the road by noon. It didn't take long to figure out that truck drivers were much more likely to stop for a party of three girls than one that included a guy with hair down to his shoulders. So Jessie, Carole, and

Marlene would prop themselves up against their bikes, blocking any view of Ed, who crouched down in the dirt. They'd stick their thumbs way out, looking tired and dejected, and sure enough, a pick-up truck, delivery van, or once, a mammoth eighteen-wheeler, would grind to a stop in the gravel just ahead of them. They'd toss their bikes in the back, stuff themselves into any available space, and arrive at the next campground well before dinner time.

It took only three days for them to make it to Oz: the Youth Hostel in Wawa, Ontario. Everyone in every bike shop in Detroit had told them about the hostel, which was just about in the middle of the TransCanada Highway, the road that connected the Atlantic and Pacific coasts of Canada. If you were hitching across Canada, man, you were on the TransCanada Highway. And sooner or later, you'd wind up in Wawa. For two dollars per night, you got a hot vegetarian dinner, use of the showers, and a mattress and pillow in a bunkhouse. Best of all, Jessie thought, you were side by side with people who were actually trekking between British Columbia and Prince Edward Island. People who knew about places called Saskatoon, Moose Jaw, and the Bay of

Fundy. Places that sounded as far from suburbia as you could get.

Places Jessie could only touch on a map.

Jessie and Marlene had just parked themselves across from Carole and Ed at one of the lunchroom-style tables that filled the hostel dining room, the walls of which were painted with rainbows and a giant lady floating on a cloud that said "Lucy in the Sky with Diamonds." It was as happy as kindergarten. Strains of Bob Dylan's "Just Like a Woman" wafted over from a corner where two guys were playing acoustic guitar and singing.

Jessie was in heaven. There was brown rice with carrots and onions in her bowl, her favorite Dylan song in the air, and everything that was Southfield far behind her. That was when she heard a deep Texas drawl in her ear.

"Y'all mind passing that soy sauce?"

She turned and saw him standing right next to her. He wore his straight tawny hair long and his beard short. Three turquoise stones hung from a rawhide strap around his tanned neck, setting off the fine chest fur that peeked out from a faded blue work shirt. His jeans were a tapestry of patches, embroidered flowers, and white cotton strings that heralded the start of yet another hole beneath his buttocks. He had a silver peace sign around his right ring finger, and he didn't wear shoes.

Jessie thought it was a good thing she was sitting down, because she could feel her legs begin to shiver. While she could hear herself saying all sorts of clever things, she managed to push only a few small words out of the back of her suddenly very dry throat.

"The what?"

With a tilt of his head and wink of his very, very blue eyes, he gestured toward the bottle of soy sauce. She handed it to him as he climbed over the bench and sat down. Right next to her.

Now her stomach began to shiver.

His name was Terry. He was twenty years old, from Amarillo, Texas, and he had been on the road for almost a year. He'd come into Canada from Seattle and was headed east, toward Nova Scotia.

"Nova Scotia. Far out," Ed said, wiping his mouth with the bottom edge of his Daffy Duck T-shirt.

"Yeah, a couple of chicks in Winnipeg told me about some big farm going on there. People living off the land

and shit. What about you people?" he asked.

"We're trucking around Lake Superior with our ten-speeds," Jessie said.

Well, that was true.

"Bikes. Far fucking out," Terry said with a slow nod of his head.

"Yeah, its pretty cool," she replied. "You get to be really in touch with what's happening, you know?"

"We go about forty miles a day. Sometimes more, sometimes a little less," Marlene said.

"Yeah, and we carry all our shit with us," said Carole.

Even Ed somehow knew to leave out the part about the trucks. They continued trading travel tales with Terry through seconds on brown rice and well into the cookies made with organic carob chips instead of chocolate. Each time Terry talked directly to her, she felt more and more, well, giddy in the head. Then Terry reached for another cookie, which jammed his leg up against hers. He leaned back with cookie in hand, but his leg never moved away from hers. Jessie waited for a very long minute and then, pretending to cough, pushed back ever so slightly. Just to make sure.

A surge of electricity tingled through her body. He

had definitely pushed back. Definitely. This grown man, this incredibly gorgeous and completely grown man, was deliberately rubbing his leg up against hers.

"Hey man, its almost eleven," Ed said, getting up from the table. "They throw you out of here at 6:30 in the morning. I gotta get some sleep."

He reached out his hand to Terry. "Take it easy, man," he said as he trotted off. His Daffy Duck T-shirt and army camouflage pants suddenly looked really stupid.

Marlene and Carole gathered the empty bowls, glasses, and forks to take up to the kitchen window. "You coming, Jess?" Marlene asked.

Terry's bare toes crept under the hem of her jeans and softly stroked the bottom of her calf. She couldn't believe it herself when she answered.

"Yeah. Listen. You guys go ahead. I'll be there in a little while."

You had to know Carole well enough to see her eyebrows shoot sky high and back in less than a second, but anyone could see Marlene's back stiffen. As Marlene's eyes sought out her own, Jessie suddenly developed an intent interest in stacking the cookie crumbs on the table into little towers.

"Y'all stay cool," Terry said.

"Yeah," said Marlene.

"Yeah, well, see you around," Carole said. She turned and whispered into Marlene's ear. Marlene smiled, but Carole launched herself into a spasm of high-pitched giggles. Jessie wondered what had gotten into Carole. She sounded like a pet monkey on a cartoon show.

"What?" Jessie asked.

"Nothing. Never mind. Oh God, that was a good one." Carole began tittering all over again as she locked arms with Marlene and sailed toward the door.

And then, they were gone.

Jessie's heart was racing. Now what?

"Hey, how about we go down to the beach and watch the Northern Lights?" Terry said.

"The what?" Jessie heard herself saying for the second time that night.

"Oh man, they're these really far out lights that dance all over the place in all different colors. You can only see them in certain places, like parts of Canada or Norway or shit like that. Come on, I'll show you."

•

Jessie sat cross-legged next to Terry, on the khaki-and-red plaid sleeping bag he had retrieved from his van, waiting for the Northern Lights to appear.

She took off her sandals and curled her bare toes in the rocky soil that was the beach off Lake Superior. Waves crashed gently against the bigger rocks that jutted into the water. A cool gust of night air blew off the lake waters, and something inside of Jessie told her to shiver long and hard. Terry picked up the cue perfectly and put his arm around her shoulders. She nuzzled into the curve of his biceps and lifted her face slightly. Just enough to tell him to meet her lips with his own.

Starlit, windswept, it was making out at its finest. Jessie had spent plenty of time in back seats, but her lips had never been this close to a moustache and beard before. Dizzy with the desire of being desired by a man, she quickly lost herself in his sweet, hard kisses and his strong embraces. Lost as his hands reached under her shirt and unclasped her bra. Lost as he gently laid her back and covered her body with his own.

Too lost to know how to make it stop. Jessie found that you could always stop a back-seat boy with a simple nudge of your hand. And start him up all over again by sliding your tongue into his mouth. Start and stop, start and stop. It was that simple. It never seemed to matter how contradictory her signals were, it was as if the body of a high school boy was completely detached from reason. She got all the kisses and cuddles she needed until someone's curfew or a policeman's flashlight signaled the end of that round.

But Terry was no boy. He didn't seem at all familiar with the sexual conventions of high school. In fact, as he began to unzip her jeans, it suddenly dawned on Jessie that Terry was intending on having sex.

Oh, my God, we're going to go all the way, she thought to herself.

Jessie figured that there were probably a lot of things you could worry about at a moment like this. Birth control. Ugly diseases that give you oozing sores. You could even find yourself more than a little frightened about what it was going to feel like to lose your virginity. For real.

But right now, she could only focus on one thing.

The tampon between her legs.

Her mind bounced back and forth like a newly sprung pinball while Terry began to slide the top of her jeans down over her hips. How was she going to get out of this? Perhaps she could turn away and murmur tearfully that she wasn't ready, like the universal heroine of those stupid stories she used to read in *Seventeen* magazine? The ones where the guy would then cradle the girl in his arms, stroking her hair and reassuring her that he would wait forever for her. Yeah, well, that wasn't going to happen, Jessie answered herself back. This is 1970; hippies are making love in parks in California and dancing naked in creeks in Woodstock. How could anyone her age not "be ready" for sex?

And if you weren't ready, how could you actually explain that to a man so many years older than you so that he wouldn't completely hate you? Forget it.

Maybe she could call the game on account of birth control. But what would happen if he had a condom in the back pocket of his jeans? Which somehow had made their way into a crumpled heap at the foot of the sleeping bag.

For a second, Jessie thought about telling him the truth. But the notion that you could talk about menstruation with a guy was, well, unthinkable. Especially one that you had just met. Never mind that the guy now had both of his hands on the elastic band of her cotton bikini panties.

Besides, Jessie argued silently, suppose she could swallow her embarrassment and tell him about the tampon. Then what? Take it out? Even if that didn't completely gross him out, where was she going to find the privacy to get the job done? Through one open eye she quickly scanned the beach. Not a building, not a tree, not even a very large rock.

So Jessie held her tongue.

And her breath.

And the sob that crawled up from the bottom of her throat. This wasn't at all what she had imagined when she had thought about losing her virginity. It didn't feel special. It felt scary. She could feel tears pooling in the corner of her eyes. Damn. One more thing she had to hide. She forced herself to open her eyes so she could quickly find something else to think about.

As Terry began to push himself inside her, Jessie saw the sky turn to fire. Long veils of pink and green glowed against the black of the night sky. She watched them dance and flicker as the hard, persistent thrusts propelled the tampon deep into her body. She thought she'd never seen anything so magical as these dancing lights and she wondered if she would need an operation to get the tampon out of her.

Jessie had one leg up on the toilet seat and was searching in desperate silence for the tampon when she heard her friends come into the women's bathroom. Through the cracks in the stall, she could see Carole and Marlene, bare-legged in the mens' extra-extra large T-shirts they all wore as nightgowns. They did the stuff girls did before bed. Putting Clearasil on your zits, tying your hair up in a ponytail. Stuff Jessie could never imagine doing again. It would be another half an hour before she would find the tampon.

The next morning, Jessie straddled the stiff leather bicycle seat and felt a sharp and fiery soreness. She would just have to push through it, she thought as she pedaled up to Carole, Marlene, and Ed waiting for her at the gates of the youth hostel.

"Hey y'all," Carole said. "Where's your cowboy?"

"'Cowpoke' is more like it," Marlene said under her breath.

"What are you talking about?" Ed said.

"Shut up, you guys," Jessie said.

Together they walked up the dirt path to the black asphalt of Highway 17. As they prepared to hit the road once again, Jessie looked back over her shoulder. The sky over the beach was clear and blue. Almost as if the whole thing had never happened. But it did, she mumbled to herself. The fire between her legs was proof of that.

"What'd you say?" asked Ed.

"Nothing," said Jessie. She took one last long look at the beach and thought about all she had lost there. "I didn't say a thing."

the uterus fairy
by Linda Oatman High

"I love my uterus," my mother blubbers. "It's where I carried you. It was your baby house. Now it's good-bye to the House of Babies. Farewell, Hotel Embryo."

"Yeah, yeah," I say. This is all we've heard around here, ever since Mom scheduled the surgery. She's having a total gutter sweep: cutting out everything female. A hysterectomy.

"If it was a tooth, I could put it under my pillow," Mom says. "I wonder if there's a Uterus Fairy?"

Dad snickers.

"Sure," he says, "she brings red Corvettes."

Mom shoots him a look.

"How would you like it," she snaps, "if your scrotum was getting cut off?"

Dad hurries out the door. I don't blame him.

"I'm going to miss my period," Mom says. She sighs. "Can you believe it, Chelsea?"

I can believe it. What Mom doesn't know is that I'm missing mine, too. It's three weeks late. I'm seventeen years old and scared to death that I might be pregnant.

Dear Journal-Girrrl. I've always thought of my journal as a girlfriend, just much quieter. It's there that I write all the stuff I can't even tell my best friend, Emily, who has a hard time keeping her mouth shut.

I'm terrified. I've never been so scared in my life. I'm freakin' petrified. Holy shit. Holy hell. Holy God. I try to deal by being funny, but this is no joke. What the hell am I going to do? Why was I so stupid? I don't love Len. I don't even like Len. In fact, I hate Len. How could I have a baby with a guy I hate? How, how, how??? Why, why, why???

Help, help, help. Please.

I'm looking back through my journal entries. Here's one from six months ago. Just six months, but it feels like a million years.

Dear Journal-Girrrl: I am so way in love!!!!!!!!!! Len is such a hunk, and he loves me, too!!!!!!! How did I get so freakin' lucky?????? We did It: went all the way. I LOVE Len!!!!

There's a huge red heart that I drew with a thick

marker, with *Len Len Len Len Len* written all around the edges. What was I thinking? Len is such a dork. I could be carrying the spawn of a dork in my belly.

My eighteenth birthday is next week. The only gift I want is my period.

I fish my cell phone from my purse and call Emily. Even though she can't keep a secret, I just have to share this with her.

"Em, this is going to sound crazy, but when did you have your period?" Emily and I are so in sync that even our monthly cycles are the same.

"You know that it was the same time that you had yours," Emily responds. "Three weeks ago. *Duh.*"

"No," I say. I take a deep breath. "Em, I didn't get it. I didn't get it this month."

There's a huge and pregnant silence on the line, and then Emily gasps.

"What are you going to do?" she says. "Get one of those early pregnancy tests or something?" Her voice is almost a whisper.

"I don't know," I reply. "I really just don't know."

We got our first periods within a week of each other,

Emily and I. We were fourteen: late bloomers. Or bleeders. Whatever. Emily and I have a lot in common: We're both late bleeders, and we both have weird mothers. Everybody else in our town has Martha Stewart moms; our mothers are the anti-Marthas. Emily and I bonded in second grade because we were the only two kids whose mothers didn't bake homemade cupcakes for the parties.

Riding the cotton bicycle. Arts and crafts week at panty camp. Playing banjo in the ragtime band. Flying the red flag. Emily's mom is the Queen of Stupid Sayings, especially when it comes to that time of the month. She actually took us to the Museum of Menstruation, which was just some wacko basement collection near Washington, D.C. It was creepy as hell: headless, legless mannequins spinning in the air, wearing different kinds of menstrual protection.

"Look, here's a U.S. Army tampon launcher," said the guy who owned the place. "Let me show you my collection of menstrual cups."

The dude even had a pink dress, for God's sake, made of hundreds of Instead menstrual cups. It was scary. If he put that dress on, I was bolting for the door.

"Let's get out of here," I whispered to Emily's mom. She ignored me. The Queen of Stupid Sayings is also the Queen of Finding Out Everything About Everything. She figured that just because we were bleeding, we wanted to know the entire world history of menstruation.

"In the Jewish culture, mothers slap their daughters across the face when they first get their period," Emily's mom said. "Something about slapping sense into them so they don't get pregnant out of wedlock, I think."

Emily and I rolled our eyes.

"What*ever*," we said.

"In the Philippines, they wipe their faces with the blood so that they don't get pimples," she said.

"Oh gross!" Emily shouted. "Thank you for sharing that."

"They also make the bleeding girl hold a cotton ball and leap three times over a blooming orchid," Emily's mom said.

"O-kay," Emily said. I just shook my head.

"The orchid symbolizes the feeling of being fresh and clean," Emily's mom said. "And the cotton ball stands for being light and airy and never burdened by menstruation.

"And Muslims don't go to church when Aunt Flo comes to visit," she said.

"Hey," I said. "Maybe I won't have to go to Mass!" We're Catholic, when Mom feels like it. It's a mortal sin to get pregnant without a husband, even though Mary did it.

And now here I am: seventeen and scared to death, praying for blood in my underpants as Mom puts her faith in the Uterus Fairy.

It's Monday morning and Emily's mother has come over for coffee and Pepperidge Farm chocolate cake. She and my mom like to get together once a month and commiserate about the stress of raising teenage girls. They also gossip about all the Martha Mothers, who try to pretend that they're so perfect. At least our mothers— Emily's and mine—are honest. They show their real selves to the world. If you don't like it, tough. Actually, it's the kind of mother I plan to be someday. A long time from now. Emily and I will be second-generation anti-Marthas. We won't cook or sew or bake or make pinecone wreaths at Christmastime. We'll ride Harley motorcycles and play rock music really loud and dress in leather and lace. We'll be the cool mothers. Someday. *Maybe sooner than later. I hope not.*

"Got some dirt for you," says Emily's mom, digging into her chocolate cake.

"Oh yeah?" Mom says. She slurps her coffee. "Diss away."

"Well . . . you know Miss Clarice, president of the PTO, perfect lipstick, helmet-head hairdo, Liz Claiborne pants Clarice?"

Mom nods. "Unfortunately," she says.

"Well, get this: Miss Clarice's perfect angel, straight-A little Miss Priss, sing-in-the-choirgirl daughter Sarah is—"

Emily's mom pauses for dramatic effect. The suspense is building. Mom leans forward. I'm interested too, because I can't stand Sarah Williams, who thinks she's so perfect.

"She's pregnant!" Emily's mother announces. Mom's jaw drops and my heart falls to the floor.

"How stupid can that girl get?" Mom asks. "I'm glad that *my* daughter has more brains than that!"

The anti-Marthas keep talking, having no idea that I've just stopped breathing and my heart is beating.

•

It's the day before Mom's surgery. No Red Flag yet.

Mom comes into my room. She's been crying, I can tell. I know the signs—puffy eyes, blotchy face—because I've been doing a lot of crying myself. Mom's holding three boxes of Tampax. I push my journal under my pillow.

"Here," Mom says. She dumps the boxes on my bed. "I won't need these anymore."

Oh, I hope that I need them.

"Just what I've always wanted," I say, "my very own Tampax collection. Maybe I could open a museum."

Mom looks at me. She doesn't find it amusing. "I'm scared," she says.

"Of what?" Moms aren't supposed to be scared.

"Of the surgery," she says. "Of somebody cutting me open. Of losing my womanhood. Even though I knew I wasn't having any more babies, I'm mourning, in a strange kind of way. It's like I'm losing something that I didn't even realize I had. Something I loved, but didn't know it until I knew it'd be gone. You know what I mean?"

Not really, but I nod.

"It's the end of an era for me," Mom says. "I'm all of a sudden looking at young girls in the grocery store and thinking, 'I bet *she* has a uterus.'"

"O-kay," I say. My mother is a certified lunatic.

"You have a wonderful gift ahead of you," Mom says.

I don't know what to say, so I don't say anything.

"I wonder if I'll look different?" Mom says. "You know, without a uterus? Maybe I'll look . . . *funny*."

I try to smile.

"Or maybe I'll have a flatter tummy," Mom muses. "That would be good."

Again, I make a lame attempt at a smile.

"I'll be taking *hormones*," Mom says. "Essence of Woman pills. Maybe I'll have facial hair or something."

"I doubt it," I say.

"It's so crazy," Mom says. "I've been getting my period for thirty years and thought I hated it. You know: The Curse. My Evil Red-Headed Uncle. But now that it's never coming again . . . well . . . I'm just going to miss it, that's all."

Me too. I'm going to miss my period. But I don't tell her that.

"You know, there were all kinds of nutsy old wives' tales, back when I was a kid," Mom says. "Stuff like you shouldn't take a bath when you're bleeding. You shouldn't wash your hair. Virgins shouldn't wear tampons."

God. Let's not talk about virgins.

"We saw this sweet little film in school, back in sixth grade," Mom says. "It didn't tell us much, except that we'd need to wear deodorant and Kotex pads. Then they gave us a little plastic bag with a sample of the stuff."

"Yeah," I say. "Things haven't changed much." That's exactly what they did when I was in sixth grade. *You're a woman now*, the mother in the movie told the girl who'd just got her period. *This means that you can have a baby.*

Being a woman isn't much fun. Just look at Mom and me.

Dear Journal-Girrrl: I can't even depend on Mom. She's scared. I'm scared. The whole world is scared. There's nothing left but scared. I'm too scared to even call the doctor, and I'm way too scared for an early pregnancy test. The truth can hurt.

•

It's the morning of the surgery. I'm leaving for school as Mom and Dad are leaving for the hospital.

"Bye, Baby," Mom says. She kisses me on the cheek. Maybe she should kiss my stomach instead, and talk to the real Baby.

I'm fat. I'm tired. I'm hungry for hot dogs. Aren't these signs of pregnancy? Plus the biggie: still no period.

Mom is pale. She's not wearing makeup or nail polish. She's not supposed to eat anything, so that she doesn't vomit during surgery. I'm feeling on the edge of puke myself.

"This is like the morning I had you," Mom says. "I was hungry, but I wasn't supposed to eat. They didn't want me to have a bowel movement during labor, you know."

"Lovely," I say. "Thanks for sharing that."

"Say good-bye to my uterus," Mom says. Lord have mercy. Now I'm supposed to kiss *her* stomach?

"It'll be fine," I say. "Everything will be just fine."

I'm trying to convince myself.

Mom's in the hospital for three days. Dad's tired. I have to do my own laundry and get my own meals. Holy crap.

There's no way I could take care of a baby: all that diaper-changing and stuff. *Please, God, let me get my period. I promise I'll never complain about cramps again. Please, please, please.* I pray this a million times a day. I go to the bathroom as much as possible, just to check my underwear. Nothing.

The three boxes of Tampax sit on my bureau, lined up like soldiers without a war to fight.

I think about Len, who burps along to songs on the radio. He picks his nose and rolls the boogers. We broke up last month. There's no way I could spend the rest of my life with somebody whose socks smell like rotten popcorn. There's no way that my baby can have a father like that. Maybe I won't even tell Len about the baby. What he doesn't know won't hurt him. What I do know is hurting me. I'd give anything to get my period. I try to will it out of me. I close my eyes and push the blood from my uterus. I open my eyes and pull down my pants. Nothing.

I look up at my bedroom wall, painted purple and plastered with posters of the lead singer of that band Creed. I zero in on one poster and talk to the guy's eyes. I pretend that he's Len.

"I wasn't going to tell you this, but maybe I should," I begin. I clear my throat. "Len," I say. I'm actually shaking, just thinking about this moment.

"Len, I'm pregnant. It's your kid."

"Are you sure?" In my mind, this is what Len says.

"Yes, I'm sure, doofus. I am pregnant and it is your kid."

"But we used condoms."

"They don't always work, stupid. Didn't you pay attention in Health class?"

"Well, did you schedule it?"

"Schedule what?"

"The abortion. Duh." Len is such a dick. There's no way I'd get an abortion. I'm *Catholic*, for God's sake.

I stare up at the poster. This isn't working. The Creed guy is way too cute to be Len. I imagine myself married to the lead singer of Creed. Cool. Then I close my eyes and picture myself married—stuck, until death—to Len. Yuck. Forget that option. I'll be a single mother.

How am I going to tell Hysterectomy Woman that she's going to be a grandmother?

Dear Journal-Girrrl: Somebody kill me, because I'm dying inside.

•

Mom is home from the hospital. She walks like a ninety-five-year-old lady, all hunched over and shuffling. She holds a pillow to her gut. She groans a lot.

"Cramps are a piece of cake compared to this," she says.

She naps a lot. When she's not napping, she's analyzing how it feels not to have a uterus.

"I can't tell yet if it's empty in there," she says. "It's not rattling or anything."

Mom pops her hormone pill every morning. I wish I'd been smart enough to pop birth-control pills. One pill a day can change everything. It can mean the difference between a baby and nothing.

It's Halloween, and there's a party at Emily's house. My costume is the Virgin Mary. It's a weird choice under the circumstances, but I guess it's wishful thinking. I'm wearing a robe (virgin white), with an old pillow strapped to my belly. Might as well get used to it. I have a sign taped onto my stomach, with an arrow pointing down and the words: *Baby Jesus*.

I'm bitchy. PMS doesn't come when you're pregnant,

does it? I would have asked Mom, but she was too grouchy.

"Hey, I like the toenails, Mother Mary," somebody says. I'm wearing sandals, and my nails are painted orange and black.

"Thanks," I say.

And then I see him: Len. The dork. The geek. The booger-rolling, song-burping, sock-stinking creep. The father of my possible baby. Lord have mercy. Let's just pretend that this was an Immaculate Conception.

Avoiding Len, I head for the Witch's Brew. Emily's mom is not only the Queen of Stupid Sayings and Finding Out Everything About Everything, she's also the Queen of Halloween. She makes this brew every year, using Pop Rocks and Sprite. It fizzles and hisses, and the ice cubes are big frozen hands. She makes them by freezing water in rubber gloves.

I scoop out some Witch's Brew. I grab a Ghost Sandwich and Skeleton Bones. I'm starving to death, and getting fatter with every bite.

"Hey, kiddo," says Emily's mom. "How's your mother feeling?"

Everybody in town knows that my mom is

Hysterectomy Woman. And if you think *that* news spread fast, wait until they find out who's having a baby. It'll probably be on the front page of the paper. Miss Clarice will announce it to the PTO. Big news in Boringville.

"Mom's okay," I say. "Still hoping for the Uterus Fairy."

Emily's mom punches me on the arm.

"No more wading the Red Sea for her," she says with a wink. "Lucky woman."

"Yeah," I say. "Lucky."

Emily's annoying little brother Kevin is sticking his sick fingers in the Witch's Brew. I still remember how he pulled a tampon from my purse one day, swinging it like a cowboy's lasso over his head. In *church*.

"Yee-haw," he said.

If I gave birth to a kid like that, I'd die.

I drink five cups of Witch's Brew, and then I need to pee. Like really bad. There's a line for the bathroom. My pillow-stomach keeps nudging the person ahead of me.

Finally, it's my turn. My eyeballs are practically swimming. I run into the bathroom, which Emily's mom has decorated for the party. It's got only a black light, and glowing posters of goblins and ghosts. There's that wispy spiderweb stuff draped from the ceilings, and a CD player with scary sounds: creaking doors and screams and all that.

I lift up my Mother Mary robe. I pull down my underpants and maneuver myself to sit on the toilet. Baby Jesus is in the way. I hitch up the pillow and pee.

When I'm finished, I look down. There's something dark in my underwear. I can't really see what it is, but the shape is like an angel. Or a ghost.

I turn on the light and brush spiderwebs from my face. The stain is red. It's here. The Red Sea. Thank you, Jesus. Thank you, Mother Mary and God and the saints and angels and the people who make Kotex. I've never been so happy to see blood in my entire life. I could almost rub it on my face, I'm so happy. Hallelujah. Thank you, Holy Ghost. Thank you, Watcher over Red Stains in Underpants.

I don't have any Tampax, and Emily keeps hers up in her bedroom. I unstrap the pillow from my stomach and throw it into the bathtub. It's ripping, and some of the cotton stuffing falls out in balls. I pick one up and stick it in the pocket of my robe.

"Good-bye to the House of Babies," I say. "Good-bye, Hotel Embryo. Hello, Aunt Flo."

I yank up my underwear. I glide out past the people in line for the bathroom. I practically dance past Len, loving the dampness of my underpants.

"What are you so happy about?" Len mutters.

"Oh," I say. "The Uterus Fairy came to visit. She brings red Corvettes."

He gives me a strange look, and I walk away. I don't look back.

I go to say good-bye to Emily and her mom.

"What, leaving already?" asks the Queen of Halloween.

"Yeah," I whisper. "Arts and crafts week at panty camp. I have to go home, where there's plenty of Tampax."

"Oh," she says, and gives me a knowing nod.

Emily squeals. "Yee-haw!" she yells, jumping up and down. We hug, and then I waltz to the door.

Stepping outside into the cool October night, I take a deep breath. Candles are burning in carved pumpkins on porches, and leaves fall, floating past my face.

I stick my hands in the pockets of the robe and find the cotton ball. *The feeling of being light and airy, never burdened by menstruation.* I'll never be burdened by the Red Flag again, I swear, so help me God. Cross my heart and hope to die. If ever I complain about cramps or PMS, just strike me dead or pregnant, God. I'll never take my period for granted again. The Uterus Fairy came to visit, and she tucked something special under my pillow. I believe in fairies, and Santa, and witches and goblins and ghouls. Magic is a cool thing, a very cool thing. We all need it sometimes.

I'm looking around for a blooming orchid, but I can't find one, so I just jump over a pumpkin instead. Three times, holding the cotton ball from Mother Mary's gut to my heart. I'm light and airy. I'm surrounded by angels and ghosts. They're even in my underpants.

I'm weightless, like air or blood or breath. I feel like I could fly. Somebody slap my face.

I'm riding the cotton bicycle and it feels like grace.

afterword
about this book and its authors
by Lisa Rowe Fraustino

when Alyssa Eisner asked me if I would be interested in editing this anthology for Simon & Schuster, my first reaction was a jolt of silent shock. My second reaction was a very long, loud laugh with my head tipped back. A collection of short stories on the theme of menstruation! What a hoot! It was bold, it was fresh, and it was long overdue. If only I could have gotten my hands on more stories about womanhood when I was thirteen and wondering if I was normal . . . when I was twenty and wondering if I was pregnant . . . when I was thirty and trying to explain menstruation to my eight-year-old daughter.

Each day when I was in eighth grade, the girls gathered on the playground in covert circles to share secret stories of their menstrual experiences. The best I could contribute was the greatly embellished tale of my little brother using my mother's pads to do the dirty deed when we had run out of toilet paper. Why had I not yet begun my period? I had passed the age when my mother started hers. Was there something wrong with me? The question dominated my mind in those days during the fall of 1974.

Day after day it seemed I wore the only unbloodied undies in all of Piscataquis County, Maine, until the big day came at last. In subsequent months the familiar red blot would become an annoyance, but that first time I rejoiced while rinsing my panties in cold water to prevent stains as Mama had taught me. Now I, too, could spend recess bemoaning how I had bled through two tampons AND a pad during a double period science lab (double *period* har har). We wore our womanhood proudly in our secret society. Cramps were our badge of honor. No boys allowed.

During my long, loud laugh while Alyssa waited on the other end of the phone for an answer, I recalled that long-forgotten recess ritual of telling period tales, recalled how desperate we all had been for understanding of what it meant to bleed, to become interested in sex, to be able to have babies: to be a woman. Yes, with pleasure, I would edit a collection of fiction about menstruation for an audience of mature young adults. And so I set to work inviting writers to contribute work from a variety of perspectives. Their stories range from comic to tragic, historical to contemporary, autobiographical to purely imaginary. I hope you enjoyed reading them as much as I enjoyed working with these talented authors.

Pat Brisson has published a dozen books, including *The Summer My Father Was Ten*, winner of the Christopher Award. She says, "I wrote 'Taking Care of Things' because I wanted to see if I could write something for an older audience, since my books are mostly picture books and easy-to-reads. Joyce McDonald suggested I use the voice that I've used in writing occasional humorous essays for my friends. That set me on the right track and the story idea came from what must be a universal concern of women everywhere—what if you get your period and can't get to a ladies room? I just compounded the situation by inventing a series of obstacles that needed to be overcome (and throwing in a love interest)."

Lisa Rowe Fraustino, editor of this anthology as well as *Soul Searching: Thirteen Stories of Faith and Belief*, teaches in the English Department at Eastern Connecticut State University, specializing in children's and adolescent literature. "I got the idea for 'Sleeping Beauty' from a newspaper article about a college student who was found dead after giving birth in a dorm bathroom, and nobody had even known she was pregnant. This situation, unbelievable yet true, raises many questions. How could a smart, talented young woman hide her pregnancy even from herself? Wouldn't she have missed her periods? My story imagines some answers and provides an implicit warning in the way that traditional fairy tales do. Women need to accept their bodies or dire consequences will result."

Joan Elizabeth Goodman began her career as a picture-book illustrator. She claims, "I wrote (with difficulty) in order to have something to illustrate. The writing eventually seduced me." Thirty books later, she has expanded from picture books and middle-grade novels to young-adult historical fiction including *Paradise*, based on a true story of survival. She got the idea for

"The Czarevna of Muscovy" from a fragment she had read about the medieval Terem in the Kremlin. "It made me wonder how those women endured their lives of confinement."

Deborah Heiligman has written fourteen children's books, most of them fiction. "Ritual Purity" is her first piece of young-adult fiction. "When I heard about the book on menstruation, my first thought was, there has to be a *mikveh* in it. I wanted to put a mainstream but troubled young woman in the Orthodox world and see how they would react to each other. When I was working on the story I had a great talk with a woman who was an Aunt Barbara for a young woman who lost her mother as a kid. She told the girl: 'You have to stop being the girl who lost her mother. That shouldn't define you for the rest of your life.' So I told that to Mimi, too, and what better way to move on than through the *mikveh* ritual? The other, deeper reason I wrote about Mimi and Barbara: I lost my own mother when I was thirty-four, and I have spent a lot of time trying to replace her. I just can't seem to do that, so I try to do it in fiction."

Linda Oatman High has published picture books, middle-grade novels, and a young-adult novel called *Sister Slam, Twig, and the Poetic Motormouth Road Trip*. She's also a songwriter and teacher of writing workshops. She says, "I wrote 'The Uterus Fairy' six weeks after undergoing a hysterectomy, wishing for my own Uterus Fairy while struggling with mixed emotions at the ending of my childbearing years."

David Lubar has the distinction of being the only male author to rise to the challenge of writing a menstruation story for this anthology. He claims it wasn't hard to find inspiration. "Several years ago, my wife and I stopped to say hi to a couple we knew, and we all decided to have dinner together. When the other guy and I headed out to pick up some food, my wife asked me to get her a box of tampons. I didn't mind, but my friend flinched. He actually didn't want to go near me in the store after I had the box in my hands." Recent books by David Lubar include *FLIP*, *Wizards of the Game*, and *Dunk*.

Michelle H. Martin is Assistant Professor of English at Clemson University. She wrote her Ph.D. dissertation on menstruation in children's literature and was invited to write the Introduction to this volume because of her knowledge about the topic. Her baby, Amelia, was born on June 12, 2003. She weighed six pounds, eight ounces, and was nineteen inches long.

Joyce McDonald is the author of several young-adult novels, from the multiple award-winning *Swallowing Stones* to *Devil on My Heels*. "The idea for 'Transfusion' came from several sources," she says, "including my own experience of working the graveyard shift in the psychiatric ward at the university hospital when I was a senior in college, and a funny story a friend told me about unleashing a whole carton of eggs at her husband during one of their more heated verbal battles. When I first began to weave together these and other seemingly disparate threads, I had no idea that the end result would be a story about the emotional distortions that sometimes accompany a colossal case of PMS."

Alice McGill was born the great-granddaughter of slaves in North Carolina. Known as a storyteller and for her historic portrayal of Sojourner Truth, she has written several children's books, including *Molly Bannaky*, *In the Hollow of Your Hand: Slave Lullabies*, and *Here We Go Round*. The story "Moon Time Child" developed from her keen interest in the everyday life of female slaves. "Drawing from passed-down stories regarding menstruation and forced breeding, I wanted to write about how young slave women protected themselves under harsh treatment. Unfortunately, very few slave women were able to save themselves from forced breeding. I am still wondering how these women viewed their babies. Perhaps that's another story."

Han Nolan has won numerous awards for her young-adult novels, including the National Book Award for *Dancing on the Edge*. She says, "I guess the seed for my story is from my own childhood. When I was in third grade and waiting in line at the water fountain, a friend of mine told me about periods and I didn't believe her, or I didn't want to. I had never heard of such a thing. She told me all girls and women get it and I thought to myself, *Well I never will.* That's as far as it went. I never tried to prevent it. The majority of the story is just from my imagination but it came from that incident and the idea of someone learning about getting periods too early and the possible consequences of that."

Dianne Ochiltree is a reviewer of children's books and the author of several books for young readers, including *Sixteen Runaway Pumpkins*. She has traced her ancestry on her father's side back to the Blackfoot tribe, and her lifelong interest in Native American cultures and customs inspired "The Women's House." "Menstruation held powerful meaning for the Lenni-Lenapes, as it did for most Native Americans. I grew up in a family of three sisters close in age, much like the spacing in Sparrow-Song's family, and I enjoyed revisiting the love, laughter, and mood swings of our sisterhood in the story. I was fortunate to have several strong women in my own family who generously gave me the support and guidance needed to make the transition to womanhood. This story helped me to honor the bond that we all have with our life mentors, and with each other."

Julie Stockler says, "Unlike the other contributors to this book, my story is not only my first piece of published fiction, it is the first piece of fiction that I have ever written. For the past thirty years, I've been a freelance medical writer, creating books, videos, articles, and Web sites for physicians. More recently I've been trying my hand at writing essays. The idea for 'Losing It' came from one of those essays. Like Jessie, I biked around Lake Superior with a pack of friends the summer after graduation. Like Jessie, I have often found myself losing my voice when it really counts. Now, for example. Even though I am going to be fifty years old and have two teenage daughters of my own, my joy in having my first piece of fiction published is seriously tempered by the knowledge that my mom and dad will be reading it."

Last week I showed my seventy-eight-year-old grandmother the forthcoming book jacket and described the theme of *Don't Cramp My Style*. She had the same reaction I had upon Alyssa's phone pitch: shocked silence followed by hearty laughter. And I realized at that moment that this book may have an even broader appeal than I had originally envisioned. Women of all ages love to tell and hear menstruation stories. We've been sharing them with each other for centuries. It's about time we started putting more of them in books.

And guys, if you're brave enough, you're invited to read them too. Welcome to the secret circle.

Lisa Rowe Fraustino
Ashford, Connecticut
July 19, 2003